A Mastery of Crows

Evelyn Flood

A Mastery of Crows
Evelyn Flood
First published by Evelyn Flood in 2024

ISBN: 9798335971775
Imprint: Independently published

Copyright 2024 by Evelyn Flood

All rights reserved. This book or any portion thereof may not be reproduced or used in any manner whatsoever without the express written permission of the publisher, except for the use of brief quotations in a book review.

Cover by Jodie-Leigh Plowman at JODIELOCKS DESIGNS

Contents

Content overview	VI
Glossary	VII
The Cosa Nostra	IX
1. Domenico	1
2. Caterina	10
3. Dante	22
4. Caterina	25
5. Luciano	30
6. Caterina	36
7. Giovanni	40
8. Caterina	47
9. Stefano	52
10. Caterina	57
11. Domenico	62

12.	Caterina	66
13.	Dante	75
14.	Caterina	81
15.	Giovanni	87
16.	Luciano	97
17.	Caterina	100
18.	Dante	105
19.	Caterina	109
20.	Domenico	114
21.	Caterina	120
22.	Caterina	124
23.	Caterina	142
24.	Dante	149
25.	Caterina	154
26.	Domenico	165
27.	Luciano	167
28.	Caterina	171
29.	Caterina	173
30.	Caterina	184
31.	Caterina	191
32.	Stefano	199
33.	Giovanni	201
34.	Domenico	204
35.	Dante	206

36. Luciano	208
37. Caterina	210
38. Dante	219
39. Caterina	223
40. Stefano	225
41. Caterina	227
42. Six months later	230
Stalk me	240
Mastery Playlist	241

Content Overview

This book contains fictional references to assault (physical and s*xual), r*pe (off page, flashbacks/PTSD), suicide, forced sterilization, drug use. violence, gore, blood, murder, alcoholism, torture, hanging/strangulation, gun injuries, use of knives, grief/loss of a child, and children.

Glossary

Nipote – Nephew

Capo dei capi – Head of the Cosa Nostra

Tentazione – Temptation

Testa di cazzo – Dickhead

Principessa – Princess

Figlio di puttana – Son of a bitch

Stronzo – Asshole

Merda – Shit

Mio caro – My darling

Buongiorno – Good morning/ good day (early afternoon)

Il mio cuore – My heart

Fratello – Brother

Madre– Mother

Buonasera – Good evening

Amore mio – My love

Grazie – Thank you
Figlia – Daughter
Cugina – Female cousin
Ti amo – I love you
Basta – Enough
Voglio passare il resto della mia vita con te – I want to spend the rest of my life with you
Resta con me per sempre – Stay with me forever

The Cosa Nostra

The Cosa Nostra

K EY FAMILY MEMBERS AND CHARACTERS OF NOTE

***

CORVO FAMILY

CATERINA CORVO

MATTEO CORVO - *CAPO DEI CAPI - HEAD OF THE OVERALL COSA NOSTRA*

*JOSEPH CORVO – *DECEASED*

MARCO DE LUCA – *CATERINA'S UNCLE*

ALESSIA CORVO – *CATERINA AND DANTE'S DAUGHTER*

***

The Crows

    Domenico Rossi – Caterina's enforcer

    Vincent, Tony, *Danny* – senior soldiers

    Nicolo Barbieri – senior solider - deceased

    Anton Maranzano – soldier – deceased

    Paul Maranzano – junior solider

    Frankie Costa – senior council member

    Alessandro fiero – junior soldier

***

Other Corvo characters

    Amie – widow of Joseph Corvo

  Aldo – *Joseph's enforcer and Amie's father – deceased*

  Bea – *Domenico Rossi's sister - deceased**

  Pepe – *Dom's brother-in-law - deceased*

***

V'Arezzo family

    Capo: Dante V'Arezzo

    Frank V'Arezzo - deceased

    Rocco – Dante's enforcer

    Vito – Dante's uncle

***

Fusco family

Capo: Giovanni Fusco

Giovanni Fusco – Gio's father

Rosa Fusco – Gio's sister

Nicoletta Fusco – *Gio's sister - deceased*

Leonardo (Leo) Romano – Gio's ex-enforcer

Johnno – current enforcer

***

Morelli family

Capo: Luciano Morelli

Paul Morelli - *deceased*

Nico – Luc's enforcer

Lucia Morelli - Luc's mother

***

Asante family

Capo: Stefano Asante

Salvatore Asante - *deceased*

Iliana Asante

Domenico

"Cat."

A small furrow appears between her brows at my murmur, but her eyes don't open.

Carefully, I tug the blue fleece blanket up, hiding her tangled mess of a dress. It's barely more than rags and blood at this point. My eyes linger on the sight of my own hands, so close to her face.

Scarred and bloody.

As we all are.

I drag my eyes over her still form again, taking her in even as I pull my hands back.

Here.

She's here, and safe, and far away from the battlefield we've left behind.

Until the next one.

Swiping a hand over my face as if I could possibly wipe away my exhaustion, I collapse into a seat opposite Dante. His fingers trace over the crumpled photograph in his hand, but he's staring out of the window, his face expressionless.

I glance down at the photo, catching a hint of bronze curls. My chest begins to tighten, and squeeze.

And then I turn my face away.

When he finally speaks, his voice is hoarse - from the smoke, maybe, or the fight. Dark traces of dried blood still fleck his face as he turns those all-too-damn-familiar green eyes on me. "She's asleep?"

At my nod, he leans forward and looks around me, as if assessing Cat for himself.

Or perhaps he's making sure she's really *here*. As if the events of tonight – or last night, by now – were nothing more than a cruel trick to tease us into believing that we might actually have won, when we have lost over and over again.

Checking on her is something none of us have been able to prevent ourselves from doing, during these last quiet hours.

She curled up in a seat and let us do it without any of the attitude I'd normally expect from her. She just... *sat* there, silent and pale in her bloody gown with her cold fingers gripping mine, even as I held onto her just as tightly. We sat there, and I stared at her as she stared out of the window, watching mutely as the pitch-black view outside slowly changed to golden shades of dawn and the world passed by beneath us.

And for the first time, I had no idea what she was thinking. What nightmares might be hiding behind those deep brown eyes.

I glance back at her again - wondering who she thinks she's fooling, with her eyes scrunched closed.

I *know* her tells, the movement of her body – I know her better than she probably knows herself. And she's not fooling me.

Nor Dante. The same awareness reflects back at me in his face, jaw tightening. He forces his eyes away, and back to me.

I wonder if he feels as helpless as I do, now there are no enemies left to fight. Not on this plane, although the tension in the air suggests otherwise.

Gripping the armrest, I force out a breath. "How much longer until we get there?"

He checks his watch. "An hour, maybe."

An hour until we land in Palermo, and the quiet peace that we've found in these hours above the sky is shattered again.

When I meet his gaze this time, my own voice is grim. "We need to regroup."

"That's what we're going to do."

It's not Dante who responds. Gio slides into the vacant seat beside mine, an empty glass dangling from his hand. He looks worse than Dante, the deep cut above his left eyebrow already knitting, even as the bruising around his eyes continues to build into a vivid purple. "But we've earned a few days to rest, Dom."

My hands tighten on the armrests. "Matteo doesn't *need* a few days. Every hour we wait is an advantage for him."

No, he needs no extra time. Not when he wasn't even part of *this* fight. Unharmed, sitting on his fucking throne in Cat's family home with his minions drinking and fucking and fighting around him.

You walked out.

The thought flips over and over in my mind, accompanied by a solid dose of guilt that settles into my stomach like lead.

I just... left. Left him there and walked away.

I could have *tried*, could have tried for Cat, but all I could think of was getting to her as soon as fucking possible.

Some fucking enforcer I am.

I wonder how he feels with his pet *killer* missing.

Gio is staring at me. When I meet his stare, he works a hand over his jaw. "We meet up with Luc. That – that has to be our priority right now."

We both carefully avoid looking at Dante. At the photograph he grips tightly.

"And then," Gio continues steadily, his tone brokering no disagreement, "We *rest*. We'll be no good to anyone if we're exhausted. We rest, we rebuild, and then – *then* we can plan."

Rest.

My hands clench tighter. I can't think of anything worse than fucking resting, than losing myself in my own thoughts.

I want to *fight*.

Want to feel blood beneath my nails, the crunch of bone. I *need* it, the pull in my veins urging me even now to pick a fight.

If I don't find a way to release the fury bubbling beneath my skin, then it's going to erupt.

Gio eyes me. My head jerks in a nod. "Where's Asante?"

Blue eyes narrow. "In the back room. Checking on his mother."

And avoiding us, no doubt.

Footsteps sound from behind me, and the man in question appears as I look over my shoulder. We all watch without trying to hide it as he leans over Cat and brushes her hair back, his broad shoulders hiding her briefly before he straightens.

He doesn't shy away from our stares. Instead, he meets them before he nods to Gio's empty glass. "Any left?"

Stefano Asante looks just as exhausted as any of us, but my shoulders tense as Gio waves a hand toward the bar lining one side of the plane. "Help yourself."

"*Grazie.*" The mutter as he brushes past us is near silent. We wait until he returns, several fingers of amber liquid filling the cut crystal glass. He throws it back like water, swallowing most of it in one before he faces us. He doesn't bother to sit, to take the empty chair beside Dante. "So."

Here we are, then. Minus one.

And I wish Luc was here, here with his fucking irreverent charm and his sarcasm to lighten the mood. Strange, to feel that need when I've spent most of the last three months desperately wishing he was anywhere but in my vicinity.

He played his role. Played the irreverent playboy to perfection, so well that we all doubted him – thought he had turned on us, on Cat, in favor of joining the *winning* side in this clusterfuck of a war.

I wonder what scars it has left on him.

I haul myself up from the chair, shrugging past Stefano to grab my own drink. I don't bother with a glass, instead gripping the neck of the bottle with my finger, and he stiffens as I push back past him to get to my seat. As if bracing for an altercation.

As he fucking should.

I have not forgotten.

I will *never* forget.

The Asante brand, burned into her fucking skin. The promise I made.

And as our eyes meet, I know he's thinking the same.

The brandy burns, and I welcome it, that little bite of pain. I take a second swig, and then a third, until Gio curses fluidly. "Steady, Dom."

Ignoring him, I pin my eyes on Stefano. "Why are you here, Asante?"

The tension jumps. Dante straightens in his seat, his eyes also landing on Stefano, even as Gio shifts his eyes between us.

Stefano doesn't look away. He meets my stare, his shoulders straightening. "Because where she goes, I follow."

Red.

The mist swoops, threatening to descend over my eyes, and I fight it, fight it with every inch of me. "You're a dead man fucking walking if you think I'm going to let you anywhere near her. Be grateful you're still alive, Asante, and that's only because you got *them* in."

I gesture to Gio and Dante as he stiffens. "Don't call me Asante."

"You're the heir now," Gio points out with a frown. "No getting away from it."

But Stefano only stares at me, dark eyes unblinking. "I don't want any fucking part of that inheritance. It can burn to the fucking ground for all I care. Have it. Take it, pick over whatever scraps are left. I *never* wanted it."

I take another swig as I survey him. I've never heard him speak so much at once, let alone with so much vehemence in his tone - have never seen his face flood with color as it does now.

"So fucking loyal," I mutter, and this time, rage crosses his face as he steps closer. Rage that almost – almost – matches what bubbles away beneath my own skin as he leans down.

"I *am* loyal to those I care about, Rossi. Caterina asked me to come, so I'm here. And the only way you'll get me to leave her side is if you put a gun to my head and pull the fucking trigger. Want to get it over with now?"

My temper erupts. "Don't fucking *tempt* me—,"

I'm out of my seat, both of us squaring off against each other. Gio jumps up as well, pushing between us with a snarled curse. "*Basta! Enough.* We have enough fucking battles. She *chose* him, Dom. Get your head around it, and quickly."

I snap my head to him, the anger rising in sweeping waves that make my hands shake as I clench them into tight fists. "She was fucking *forced* into it. Where's the choice in that?"

Whatever Caterina was forced to do to stay alive while she was buried in that fucking hellhole - whatever she felt she had to do, to *say*, to survive it – I'll be fucking *damned* if I let him hold her hostage over it for a moment longer.

Not when I have failed her so badly already.

But Gio shakes his head at me, and there's something in his expression - something like pain, that makes me pause.

"Stefano *got her out*," he says quietly. His hand is on my shoulder, squeezing, gripping as if he would hold me in place in case I go for the asshole's jugular. "I was *there*, outside the walls, waiting for her. I saw her, spoke to her. But she wouldn't – *she wouldn't leave*. She went back, Dom. There was no coercion. She chose to walk back inside the Asante compound, and nobody forced her."

My eyes dart to his. She *wouldn't*—

"She went back." Gio hesitates, then. "For *him*."

My eyes slide to Stefano's face. And it's twisted, twisted in something that looks remarkably like the agony lacing my own chest.

"I wish she had left," he rasps, his eyes on mine. And there's disbelief there, as he shakes his head. "But he's right. She came back. She would not leave me, and she wouldn't risk Alessia. And the *cost*—,"

A hole opens up in my chest as his voice stutters over that word.

His voice hardens. "I will not leave her now. Whatever follows."

I have to close my eyes.

She went back.

"So," Dante says quietly. "Then there were five."

I tear my eyes away from Stefano to glance at him in question. He waves his hand. "Five men, including Morelli. Unless we're expecting any more?"

There's a twist in his voice. Something harsh, but it's *me* he's staring at as if he wouldn't mind giving me the fight I feel so desperate for.

"What?" My tone borders violence.

He only raises a mocking brow at me. "I'm only checking. Any more arrivals we should know about? What about *added extras*? Do I have any other children you've *hidden* from me, Domenico? Or was it only my daughter you lied about?"

The others still.

Dante's sharp blow lands with all the more power behind it for the unexpected question. I rock back on my heels as if it were physical, taking in the fury he finally allows to show on his face now that we're all out of immediate danger.

Another reckoning to face.

And I knew it was coming, knew that I would need to answer for this too - but fuck if I'd nearly forgotten amidst the pain of everything else these last few months. And that guilt wraps itself around my neck with a throttling grip.

Whatever friendship we started to build... I see none of that reflected in his face as he stands, his fingers adjusting the fit of his suit jacket, even though it's covered in soot and ripped on the one side.

This is the V'Arezzo capo. Cold, and angry, and right to be. I have no defense, aside from protecting Cat.

And she will *always* be my first priority.

"Dante—,"

There's an apology, low and genuine, in my voice. Or the beginnings of one. The words I owe him are too big to fit within a single sentence, and too fragile for me to share them here, with everyone watching us.

But his own anger is too strong to allow me anything at all, and I can't fucking blame him for it as he steps closer. I don't move, even as his finger stabs into my chest.

"You're itching for a damn fight, Domenico." I jerk at that, but he doesn't let up, his words a low snarl. "I can fucking see it – *all* of us can see it. And I'll happily fucking give it to you, but *not here*. If I can hold onto my need to punch you in the fucking face for keeping my *daughter* a secret from me, then you can sit the fuck down until we get off this plane and get her somewhere *safe*."

His words drop to a hiss as he glances behind me.

We all turn, as if all of us are synced to the woman who brought us together in the first place.

But her eyes stay closed, even as that furrow in her brow remains.

Awake, but silent.

And Caterina says nothing.

CATERINA

I can feel their eyes on me as the tension around us rises, threatening to spill over into something physical as Dante and Domenico face each other, their words carrying.

They're all watching. Waiting - for something, anything. For me to jump up, to pull them apart, to give them a sharp tongue and sharper wit.

But I don't give them anything. I *can't*.

All I can do is breathe.

Keep breathing.

In, out.

Again.

Again.

And the ice – that cold, numbing sensation that crept over my body as I walked out of the Asante compound for the last time – it steals all of the words that I might have said to them, strangles them in my throat as I lay here with my eyes closed, listening but numb.

So fucking numb.

There is so much to do, so much to say – to all of them. And I don't know where to start. Where to look first, to try and fix our broken pieces.

So instead, I breathe.

***

"Cat." Warm hands are gentle on my cold skin, pushing back my hair. "We're here."

The popping in my ears told me that already. We've landed in Palermo, the brightness against my closed eyelids telling me that it's morning, or something close to it.

I need to get up. To unlock my aching muscles and sit *up*.

Move.

It physically hurts. I'm so *tired*, the exhaustion weighing me down as I force my eyes to open and meet Stefano's dark gaze.

Even that requires effort. As if I have to tell my body what to do, or else it will not move at all.

His lips tighten as he scans my face. But his voice is soft. "You ready?"

My head jerks up and down, and he looks as if he's going to say something. But he hesitates. "I need to get my mother."

Iliana. I thought of her too, as I was laying here, pretending to be asleep to avoid the conversations I need to have.

I wondered if she felt as I do now, before she decided to block the world out completely. Wondered what the final straw was, that broke her spirit, that took her from a vibrant, happy woman to an empty shell.

I wondered if her straw was the same as mine.

A black canopy.

A bare back.

Cold hands on my skin—

Stefan looks relieved as I nod again, blinking those thoughts away. Plenty more rush in to take their place. I mentally force my limbs to uncurl, sensation rushing back in burning pulses as I push myself upright, the blanket that Dom pulled over me falling away as I look down.

Blood. Dried, flaking blood covers me, covers the pale material I dressed in to please my husband before I ended him.

I can't leave the plane like this. "I need something to wear."

They all stop at my words. Even my voice doesn't feel like mine. Empty, monotone.

Gio steps up beside Stefan with a hooded sweatshirt in his hands and an apology in his eyes. "We don't have much else until we get there."

"There?" I take it from him and pull it over my head, dragging it down to cover the tattered remains of my gown.

He purses his lips. "The Morelli estate."

My fingers clench in the material, so warm against my cold skin that I wonder if he pulled it off himself before giving it to me. Slowly, I nod in understanding.

Luc.

And—

Brushing away those thoughts too, I force a small smile to my face, as if it could possibly fool anyone. Gio watches me steadily. Dom moves past him to take my hand again. Gripping it tightly, as if he'd hold me together by that alone.

They wait for me. "Let's go, then."

Gio handles the arrangements as I walk off the plane, going ahead and murmuring to the men waiting for us. The airstrip is small. Private. Probably for the best, considering we all look as though we should be arrested on sight.

The warmth of the Italian dawn kisses my skin as Dom makes his way down the metal flight of stairs in front of me. A light breeze dances across my cheeks as I pause at the top and take a deep breath.

And another.

Behind me, fingers brush against my back, and I stiffen. Dom glances over his shoulder at my delay, and I move forward without looking behind.

Not yet.

"Caterina. *Please.*"

Ignoring the low voice – ignoring the pain there that threatens to crack open the numb shell encasing me - I keep my eyes down, following Dom's lead as he moves toward one of the two black cars waiting for us.

He pulls the door open, holding it, and I slide inside, into the air-conditioned space.

And I wait.

Listening to the muttering coming from outside the car, low voices raising and falling as I sit silently.

And then a familiar warmth brushes against me, as someone else gets in. I wait, but nobody else joins us. Instead, the door in front of me opens and closes.

Dom's steel-gray gaze meets mine through the small gap that separates us. He's not in the back with me, instead choosing the front passenger seat. Dom moves his eyes between my face and the window that would block him out.

Offering us privacy, for this conversation that I can't escape any longer.

No, I want to say. *Leave it open. Please.*

I am not ready.

But I nod. Breathe in again as he pushes that window shut, sealing me in.

With Dante.

I have not seen him since that night.

One hundred days without him, and I can't even *look* at him.

We've been driving for several minutes when he breaks the heavy silence. "*Tentazione.*"

I try. Try to reach for something, anything. But the panic curls around my throat, constricts my oxygen, wrapping around my lungs until it's all I can do to *breathe*.

And he stiffens as my ragged breathing becomes audible. Rasping, choking breaths fill the space between us with my panic.

I have spent so long refusing to think of the possibility of this moment that I *can't*.

Can't speak.

This is my reckoning. The moment where I face him, where I lose him, for the lies I told over and over again.

He gave me his love, his passion, his loyalty, *everything* that makes Dante V'Arezzo who he is. And what I gave him in return... it was only ever a smokescreen, and now we both know it.

I made a choice, and it wasn't him. It was *her*, always her.

Alessia.

Our daughter.

The closed window in front of me wavers, blocked by Dante's face as he rips off his belt and slides to his knees in front of me. He cups my face, his breathing almost as ragged as mine.

"*Tentatzione*," he breathes. And his voice – it threatens to break, as he stares at me. "Talk to me. *Please*."

It *does* break on that final plea, and the liquid swimming in my eyes spills over, trickling down my cheeks as I inhale. "I...,"

I'm sorry.

I'm so sorry.

But nothing comes out as he scans me with those green eyes. He has always seen me. But now, he looks at me as if he's trying to see past the Caterina he *thought* he knew. As if he has realized that maybe he never knew me at all.

As if we are strangers, he and I.

And that thought hurts.

I'm sorry. I'm so sorry.

But my lips don't move as I stare at him blindly. My tears soak into his hands as he cradles my face, his dark brows drawing down in agony.

He rips his hands away, and I brace for it. For the judgment. The anger – all of it, deserved, for the truth I kept from him, all this time.

You kept her from me.

You lied to me.

I deserve his censure. Because I didn't tell him. Didn't tell him when I found out, didn't *trust* him. Instead, I ran to my father rather than trust the man who should have been my enemy, and that single decision has cost us both more than I can ever voice.

His harsh breathing fills the car as he grabs my hand. Dante untangles my clenched fingers and pushes something into them.

I blink away the moisture blurring my vision as I look down, smoothing the image with trembling fingers.

And I stare at it for long minutes. As my shaking increases, as drops of liquid land on the picture of the little girl grinning at me.

His voice is thick, as his hand returns to my face. He traces my cheek with the tips of his fingers, smoothing away the tears.

"Look," he whispers finally. His voice is low. Emotional, as Dante V'Arezzo and I face the truth together at last. As he forces me to face the truth of us, and of her. "Look what we made, *tentazione*. Look how beautiful she is."

My sob breaks out, and he keeps talking. Keeps breaking me, ripping down all of the defenses that I spent months building against him, one by one as they collapse like dominos.

All that time, always fighting to keep them up, even when he wouldn't let me go.

"Look at our daughter," he whispers. "She has your curls, and my eyes, Caterina Corvo. She's *perfect*."

My throat is burning with the force of my tears as I grip that photograph.

"And she's safe." Fierce words as he grips me. "You did that, Cat. You kept her safe. You did everything you could, and now she's safe. Luc got her out, but you kept her safe."

My whole body crumples, but Dante catches me. His arms wrap around me as I bury my face in his neck. His hand slides into my hair, holding me tightly as I let it all out.

The words tear from my throat, rasping and hoarse. "I should have told you."

"Yes." He knows what I mean. "You stubborn, *infuriating* woman."

I suck in a breath – possibly of agreement – but he's not done.

"I understand, Cat." I don't argue when he reaches to undo my belt, when he pulls me down and twists us so I'm positioned on his lap on the floor, his arms tight around me.

My fingers dig into his wrists where he holds me as I listen, letting him say everything he needs to.

"I know why you wouldn't have told me at first. But after, Cat, after you came back – when we were building this, you should have told me. We should have faced it together, you and I. You chose to do it alone rather than trust me to stand by you. I didn't understand why you always kept me at a distance, always pushed me away, always kept that damn wall up, and now I know. And I'm furious with you."

There's hurt there. Hurt that I caused.

"I didn't know how." I study the floor of the car as I admit it, staring at the dark plastic mats with evidence of boot marks stamped into them as I search for the words. "I kept it in for so long, Dante, and then – I didn't know how to tell you, where to even begin. It was easier to keep fighting, keep arguing. And my father, he was *watching*."

Always watching. Always, I had to walk that line.

"She was a hostage," I say hoarsely. "To keep me in line, and I didn't have a choice because I would never have risked her safety. For so long, I wouldn't even let myself think of her. Even now, it's hard."

Even now, my mind slips away from thoughts of her name.

Our daughter has been a hostage since the day she was born.

First, to my father.

Then, to Matteo.

But no longer.

Dante takes a breath. There's fury on his face, twisting his features into something savage. "*Never again.*"

And my own voice is hard as I stare back at him. Soaking in the determination there, the fierce protectiveness in those green eyes that threatens to break my heart all over again, because I denied him this. "No. Never again."

Never again will she be used against us. I can read it in his face, feel it in the fire that flickers to life in my own chest, when I wondered if it would ever burn again.

No more secrets between us.

And our daughter will never be a pawn in the games of the Cosa Nostra again.

Fingers brush my skin as he takes a deep breath, swallows. "I'm still pissed at Rossi."

At the lie that cleaved apart the friendship they were tentatively building.

"He did it for me. And for her. You cannot forgive me and not him." Then, I pause, that fear tightening my chest again. "Unless—,"

"Yes," he says simply, answering my unspoken fears without hesitation. "Yes."

I have to close my eyes. His forgiveness, given so easily without question or reservation.

Fuck, but I never stood a chance against this man. All those months of pushing him away, keeping him at arm's length even as he slotted into my life and my bed. As much as I pushed, he always pushed *back*.

Dante V'Arezzo was never going to walk away from me.

And I'm done with walking away from him.

He squeezes my wrist in acknowledgement, or admonishment. "I'll work it out with Dom. But no more lies, *tentazione*. We're starting again, you and I. No more hiding from me. Please."

Slowly, I nod. "No more lies."

No more hiding.

Dante's fingers dip beneath my chin then, lifting it as he examines my face. "I'll only ask once. Is there anything else?"

I watch him. Take in the creases in the corners of his eyes, the faint lines on his forehead that weren't there a few months ago. The deep circles beneath, the stubble that he hasn't bothered to shave away.

He's not a boy anymore. We age young in the Cosa Nostra, age through violence and death, and the evidence of it is there for me to see on Dante's face.

As it is on all of us.

His eyes threaten to shutter as he reads my expression. "Tell me."

This truth.

This last, final truth.

I wet my lips, forcing myself to voice the words I kept hidden, even from Dom. The final truth of those hours and days after my daughter was taken from me.

The truth that remained voiceless, even through my time at the Asante compound. Through the horrific, invasive hours I spent with Reed and Salvatore as they investigated my body, assessing it, discussing it as I lay there, trapped and tied and holding onto that thought with *everything* I had.

Because there was one thing they did not check. One test that would have changed everything, if they had thought of it.

But they did not. And I held that thought, held it even as I woke up to fractured memories of a black canopy and bare skin.

My breathing starts to speed up.

Warm fingers, then, on my face, tracing my skin. Infinitely gentle. "Come back to me."

I blink, clearing those thoughts away as Dante's face replaces them. And I keep my eyes on his as I let those words free.

"My father... after I had Alessia. He had my tubes tied, Dante."

A precaution, he had said. *To prevent any future issues.*

But we both knew it was another punishment.

There will be no siblings for Alessia. Not from my body, at least. None of them, these men that have given so much for me, none of them will ever see me that way, never see my body change and develop as it did in those months, *before*.

That choice has been stolen from me, from all of us.

There will be no more heirs from the Corvo line, if we win against Matteo.

And in the Cosa Nostra, where family is *everything*... maybe that changes things.

Dante sucks in a harsh breath, his face paling. "*Cat*."

I try to drop my eyes from his, but he grips my face, holding me in place as he examines my expression, his brows knotting. "Do you think I care about that? About any of it?"

"It matters," I say numbly. "There will be no heirs, Dante."

None, except for Alessia. And it only puts more of a target on her head.

He pulls me closer, and I let my head rest against his chest. He traces the flecks of blood that still speckle my skin, traces the space beneath my eyes, space that I know is dark with evidence of my own nightmares. Of these past few months without him.

"I hate that he did that to you," he says finally. His voice is dark, threaded with anger. "I would kill Joseph for it, Cat, if he were here. For him to take that choice from you is unforgivable. But it changes *nothing* of how I feel about you, *tentazione*. And the others will feel the same. There are options we can explore, if and when *you* want them. And if that day never comes, then it *does not matter*."

My eyes squeeze closed, the relief soaking into my bones at the absolute honesty in his voice. "One less thing to worry about, at least."

And he freezes, as I realize what foolish words I have let free about the time we spent apart. Both of us still, tension threading around us.

And I listen as his breathing turns ragged beneath my cheek, as his heartbeat thunders.

Whatever he might have expected, I have just confirmed it.

"*Cat.*"

Dante's eyes are darker than I have ever seen them when I look up. His skin is bunched tight around those eyes, those eyes that are glimmering with something darker than I've ever seen them. His hands tighten on me, then loosen immediately. "*Quel figlio di puttana.*"

And his voice *breaks* on those words. His mouth opens—

"Don't," I force out, my voice thickening as my heart thumps heavily inside my chest. "Don't ask me anymore. Not yet. *Prego*, Dante. Don't make me lie to you when I've just promised not to. I'm *here*. It doesn't matter."

There I go, already breaking my promise not to lie to him again. Because it does matter, and we both know it. But he doesn't call me out.

He closes his eyes instead, pain in every crease of his face, and I do the same as he lowers his forehead, pressing it against mine. Our breathing mingles together.

"It matters. *Ti amo.*" His lips move up, press against my head. "*Ti amo*, Cat. No matter what."

Dante

My eyes are burning.

Leaking with anger and pain and sheer fucking agony.

She's here and safe in my arms, the truth finally out between us.

No more lies.

And the truth, the horrors that she has shared with me, they swipe the oxygen from my lungs, threatening to drag darkness over my eyes as I pull her to me and bury my face in her neck.

They, *they*— what they have done to her—

I loosen a shuddering, pained breath. And Cat – she sinks her fingers into my hair, grips it. Holds me to her, anchoring me in place as if she is the one doing the comforting when I should be doing that for her.

How much can a person be expected to endure without breaking?

How much fucking more will she be forced to endure before this is over?

I hold her even more tightly at the thought of that, as I murmur my own truth against her skin.

I am hers.

Caterina Corvo owns me. Has always owned me, body and soul and heart, even if she's now sharing it with a little girl that's a perfect mix of her and I.

And I cannot think of the truth she just brushed away. Of what happened to her behind those walls, in that horror of a fucking compound.

If I think of it, then I will burn. Turn to fire and ashes and there will be nothing left of any of us, if I go on a rampage to try to clear this pain from my body.

Too long. We took too long.

She chose to go back in when she could have run, and there was a price to pay.

A price that she does not wish to speak of. So I let it slide, that one hideous truth, and instead of forcing her to face it I whisper against her skin the words that I've been holding in since she ran toward me through a hail of bullets.

Words that I've held close for months, waiting for my *tentazione* to come home.

"*Ti amo*, Cat. No matter what."

I'm not expecting a response. I've never received one, never thought I *needed* it.

At this moment, though, I realize that I do need it. Desperately.

And I'm not expecting what slips from her mouth as she lets me hold her, her fingers gripping me tightly in a way she never has before – in a way that I'm not sure she's even aware of.

I have told her I love her more than once. Never expecting to hear it back.

But her quiet, fervent whisper closes my throat entirely. "*Ti amo*, Dante V'Arezzo. I should have said it a long time ago."

I inhale raggedly. "Say it again. Please."

Her lips brush my cheek, kiss away the wetness there. "*Ti amo. Voglio passare il resto della mia vita con te*, Dante."

"*Resta con me per sempre*," I breathe. "Don't leave me again, Cat."

I cannot be separated from her again. Never again. I would not survive it.

And it's not fair to ask her; not when we cannot control it, but I do anyway. "Promise me. Please."

She has made promises before, but never to me. This is the promise I ask of her.

Don't leave me. Stay with me.

And her tears mingle with mine as we grip each other in the back of that car.

"*Sì*. I swear it."

CATERINA

The silence that surrounds us in the back of this car is peaceful, rather than tense. A silence that speaks of relief, and truth, and the feel of being together again after so long apart.

And I find myself reluctant to break it as I glance out of the window. Dante tightens his hands, still wrapped around me, at my movement. He leans forward to follow my look. "Morelli's a fucking show-off."

The corner of my lip barely twitches at his dry words as he scans the villa that rises up in front of us behind the security gates. But the fact that a smile threatens at all—

Little steps.

I need to remember who I am. To find myself again - that Corvo heir, the Crow, and I need to do it quickly.

I do not have time to mope, to lose myself in everything that has happened.

Instead, I take another breath.

I'm here.

I'm free.

Nothing else matters.

Maybe if I tell myself that enough, if I push away those fragments of memory every time they threaten to overtake my mind... maybe I'll start to believe it.

Dante runs his hand over my back as the car slows to crawl through the gates that instantly close behind us. "Are you ready?"

The refusal hovers on my tongue.

No, I am not ready.

I'm not ready to meet my daughter. To look Alessia full in the face, to see the shared features that shine out so clearly on her face.

Today, I can feel her in my arms without the heaviness of everything they used to keep her from me weighing down my soul.

My chest constricts as I tip my head up to meet Dante's gaze. "I wouldn't let myself think of this moment. Not often. It just... it made everything so much harder. But when I *did*... I always thought that Bea would be there."

I can imagine her so clearly. The way that she would step forward with a warm welcome, the way she would help us all adjust with gentle words and a no-nonsense attitude in that *way* she had – that way that made her my first and only choice for my daughter's guardian.

And the thought is almost unbearable, the realization smashing into me once again as I turn my eyes toward the closed window - to where Dom sits quietly, giving us this space even as he nurses his own grief.

Because his sister, the only family that Domenico had left - she will not be there. Bea and Pepe are gone, murdered by Matteo and his men. Their small but strong family, broken and shattered in one hideous night.

"She was so good," I whisper. And my voice breaks. "I don't know how to do any of this, Dante. Bea was... she deserved to be Alessia's mother. And Alessia deserved to have someone like Bea."

She deserves a mother who knows what she's doing.

And me? I have no idea how to do any of it. Give me a gun, or a knife. Those are easy – but a living, breathing tiny human... she deserves better than me.

None of this is fair. None of it.

Dante's heartbeat thuds against my ear. "You don't think you can be a good mother?"

I suck in a shuddering breath. "I think that the Cosa Nostra isn't a world that I would ever want to raise a child in. I always expected to have children eventually... I suppose. One day, in the future, once I had done everything I needed to."

When I was the Corvo capo, perhaps. When I had built the empire I wanted, the empire that would keep our family strong for generations to come with me at the helm. I would have married a man who suited the needs of the family, no doubt nudged by my father, if not outright bargained away. Would have matched with someone for the power they could give me and given him children to bind the agreement in full.

How stupid I was.

And how blind, to think I could be happy with that, when these men exist.

"But not yet," I force the thought away and focus on Dante's face. "Not now, when there is so much to do."

His nod is slow.

"These things rarely happen as we plan them," he says quietly. "Sometimes too soon, sometimes too late, and sometimes never. None of us are perfect, *tentazione*. *You* do not have to be perfect. We will all need to adjust, to learn what life will look like with Alessia in it."

He strokes his thumb across my face. "She deserves a mother who loves her, Cat. No more, no less."

I can't stop the flinch.

His voice gentles. "And she has that. She has *always* had it, from two strong, brave women, and everything else does not matter in the face of that."

I stare at him, drinking in those words that warm up the ice still gripping my heart even as he shifts, lifting me back onto the seat as the engine cuts out. I'm still silent as the car door swings open and he climbs out.

A tanned, tattooed hand appears. An offering.

"Together," Dante says quietly as his face appears. "We will face this together, Caterina Corvo. And I will be with you, as I should have been from the beginning."

Together.

Another breath.

And then I reach out, and take his hand.

Dante wraps his fingers around mine, solid and warm as I step out of the car and look around. "Where did the others go?"

"Stefano and Gio got here before us. They went ahead, and Dom followed."

Dante's eyes are already on the large set of carved wooden doors, open to reveal a shadowed entrance hall. I catch a glimpse of brightly colored rugs covering gray flagstones before a silhouette fills them, blocking out the view.

A familiar silhouette, shadowed from the sun.

And as my breath catches in my lungs, he steps out into the bright morning light and holds up his hand to get a better look.

Luciano Morelli grins at me. There are shadows there, shadows behind his eyes and evident in the purple beneath them, but he raises one eyebrow at me as if we're nothing more than the mocking rivals he pretended we were - pretended so well, for so long.

But his eyes are bright, suspiciously so.

"Little crow. You're late."

And if his voice breaks, none of us mention it.

Because I'm already running.

Luciano

"Aiiieeeee!"

"*Fu—*,"

Diving in, I swipe the razor from Alessia's hands, tapping her gently on the nose. "Trouble. I called it the second I saw you, *cuoricino*."

I get a dazzling, gappy grin in response to the gentle chastisement, before Alessia throws herself back into my bag, dragging out my clothes and tossing them everywhere. A loud peal of laughter rings out as I grab her, tossing her up in the air to distract her as she cackles at me.

"Now then," I say seriously. I settle her into the crook of my arm as I turn to the door. "Remember what we talked about. No cheek grabbing. No nose biting. And definitely no *accidents*."

I wince, glancing over my shoulder at the rapidly depleting supplies. "Please, no accidents. This is your last clean outfit until tomorrow."

The last twenty-four hours have been an… adjustment, to say the least. We arrived home to an empty house, the staff sent on a paid break and my mother booked into the finest spa Sicily has to offer for the next two days.

Space for us to breathe. To recover.

I glance down at the little girl in my arms. She buries her head into the crook of my neck, her breathing tickling my skin as I carry her down the steps. Ahead of us, engines rumble before cutting out, leaving silence in their wake.

My stomach swoops, heavy and tugging as I grip Alessia that little bit tighter. Run my hand over her curls, reassuring myself. "Everything is going to be fine."

I don't know who I'm talking to. I step out onto the flagstones, my feet eating up the space as Alessia starts to wriggle, indignant noises coming from her mouth as she throws herself to the side.

"Steady, mini crow." I let her slide down to the ground where she promptly begins to tug at the pretty threads in the rug, crouching to balance her as footsteps ring out.

Swallowing, I stand to face the man who walks in first. "Gio."

"Luc." Gio looks battered, a nasty cut on his forehead as he strides toward us. He scans Alessia, his eyebrows raising as he takes her in, the stern slant of his mouth softening. "She's Caterina's double."

I only nod, my attention moving back to the front door. Alessia looks Gio up and down before ignoring him completely in favor of the carpet, and he huffs in amusement before turning back to me. "I wouldn't mind washing up. There a shower in this place?"

I wave a hand toward the stairs. "Hell of a lot of bedrooms here, *fratello*. Take your pick. Most of them have spare clothes that should fit you."

"*Grazie.*" Gio hesitates, then. His blue eyes scan my face. "How are you doing?"

I'm not sure the sardonic smile I offer him fools either of us, but it slips effortlessly into place. "I'm not the one who walked off a battlefield and came straight here. First aid kit's in the kitchen. Don't want to scar that handsome face of yours."

I nearly miss Gio's quiet response as he moves past, gripping my shoulder before he heads up. "You sure about that?"

Stefano is next, escorting a quiet, pale woman with the same dark eyes. He nods at me when I murmur directions to a suite down the hall, my eyes scanning the familiarity of her features. Despite her relative youth, she shuffles as if her entire body is on the verge of giving up, her eyes not meeting mine as she stares at the floor and grips her son's arm.

"*Benvenuta, signora*," I say carefully, but she still shrinks away. Stefano meets my gaze with an apology in his eyes, but I shake my head in dismissal. I'm well aware that I'm not the problem, and my body tightens in anger again before I force my muscles to unclench.

"There's a room next door to the suite." I keep my voice quiet, addressing Stefano. "Does she need anything in particular?"

He shakes his head even as his dark gaze drops, taking in the little girl playing on the rug. "Just a quiet space and some rest. Thanks, Morelli."

I watch them go with a slight frown. Tiny fingers grip my cream chinos, and I glance down as Alessia pulls herself up with a slight wobble. She lets out a victorious noise, waving her fist around, and I have to smile.

She takes a few wobbling steps and lands firmly back on her backside with a bump. My half-step, half-jump in her direction goes unnoticed as she laughs, her fingers digging back into the rug.

I blow out a breath, turning toward the front door before I stop.

Domenico Rossi.

Swallowing around the lump in my throat, I cross my arms. "You managed to get away, then. Glad you could make it."

Slowly, he nods. His eyes fall to Alessia, and something like devastation flickers across his face before he returns his attention to me, his voice low and abrupt.

"How much of it was real?"

I pause. "Not in the mood for chit-chat, then?"

But I know what he's asking. How much of my soul did I rip away in those months laughing beside Matteo? Exchanging little pieces of my self-respect for just the *possibility* of the little girl in front of me? How much of me is left?

How much of Domenico Rossi is left?

"Too much," I say finally. Honestly. "And I would do it again, Dom."

I would do worse – far fucking worse - if it meant getting Alessia away from there. And the guilt sinks cold claws into me once again at the memory of Amie racing back through that tunnel, racing toward Matteo to buy us time to run.

She bought Alessia's freedom with her own safety.

"Amie," I say roughly. "Did you see her?"

Slowly, he shakes his head, brows creasing. "Matteo was looking for her when I left."

I run a hand over my face at the implied question. "She could have gotten out. But Matteo would have noticed her absence long before Alessia's. So she stayed, and went back to him."

Silence. "Seems to be a lot of that going around."

At the sharp words, my own brows knot. But he brushes past me, going out of his way to avoid crossing paths with the little girl at my feet. "Dom—,"

"Not now," he says hoarsely. "Where can I go?"

I watch him. Watch the way he holds himself, as if ready for a fight. The way he's had to hold himself for months, night after night of fighting and killing for Matteo's entertainment. "Straight up the stairs. Pick any of the empty rooms."

He doesn't respond, his feet eating up the stairs as I slowly turn back to the door. When nobody else appears, I take a few more steps.

I need to see her.

Need her.

And I raise my hand up against the morning glare, squinting at the two people next to the car. Dante nods at me, but Cat... Cat's face starts to crumple.

"Little crow." My voice is hoarse. "You're late."

My voice is thick, my throat tightening. And Cat—

She launches herself toward me, her feet eating up the distance between us as she runs straight to me and I throw my arms around her, dragging her to me and gripping the back of her head as she buries herself into me.

I breathe nonsense into her ear, a garbled mix of Italian and English as I hold onto her.

I hold onto her as tightly as I can, and it feels as though my lungs have filled with air for the first time in months.

I can finally *breathe*.

I don't move until she does, my hands reaching up to cup her face. I don't hide that I'm examining her, the memory of her empty face still able to paralyze my throat with fear. Caterina closes her eyes, her hands moving to cover mine. "I'm okay, Luc."

No, she's not. I know it, and so does she.

"You will be," I say quietly. My thumb strokes over her cheekbone, just once, before I draw away and meet Dante as he steps forward.

I glance down at his outstretched hand, reaching out to grip it. "Welcome."

He nods, his grip tightening as he looks over my shoulder and back to me. "Luc – is she—,"

"Here," I breathe, and he freezes. "Right inside the entrance."

And Dante V'Arezzo pales. His hands drop, tugging at the cuff of his shirt as if trying to make himself presentable in his battered clothes. "I see. Cat...,"

She slips beneath my arm, fitting there like a puzzle piece. Her brows are scrunched when I look down, tight with worry and something deeper.

My smile feels crooked. "Do not worry. Your daughter is *very* forgiving of mistakes, I have found."

A small sound of amusement slips from Dante's mouth as he holds out his hand to Cat. "Together, then, *tentazione*?"

I let her go as she slips her hand into his. She glances at me over her shoulder, her eyes soft.

"Together."

CATERINA

My legs begin to tremble as I take a step. Another.

Behind me, Luc stays still. I look back at him and then to Dante. He still grips my hand – to settle his own nerves as much as to steady me, perhaps, but he offers Luc a nod. "After you, Morelli."

Luc straightens in surprise, and I offer him a small smile. "Lead the way."

Together.

Luc's hand dances across my back before he steps forward and ducks into the hall. I force my shaking legs to move after him, Dante close behind me as we step through into the cool shade.

Luc twists, a low curse escaping him. "She's fast."

Dante steps up beside him as I hang back. "She was here? Where did she go?"

And just like that... two of the strongest men I know dissolve into panic.

They both spin, searching the empty room before Luc sprints for the stairs and Dante heads down one of the corridors leading from the hallway. Their voices bounce back at me as they call for Alessia.

Turning in place slowly, I scan the floor. And my heart stumbles inside my chest as I catch sight of a pair of tiny bare toes, tucked away behind the door. A low giggle slips out, and the toes curl before disappearing from my sight.

I take one, single step. Another.

And I drop to my knees, gently pulling the door away from the wall as my heart swoops into my stomach. And my voice – it shakes as I whisper the words around the lump growing in my throat. "Hello, Alessia."

My daughter smiles at me. A big grin, showing off the several teeth growing there. Her hands slap against the floor as she looks at me, those emerald-green eyes making my own suspiciously misty as she opens her mouth.

A long, unintelligible babble of words spill out. She stares at me, as if waiting for a response.

I can't speak.

I can't do anything but take in the sight of my daughter, dusty and happy and dressed in a little green sundress with bare feet. Her bronze, untamed curls bounce around her head as she awkwardly pushes onto her knees and then *up*, gripping the door.

She takes a single, wobbling step. Another, until she's right in front of me, and she lets go of the door in order to grab my outstretched arm instead.

I choke out something that might be a laugh as she pulls herself closer, examining my face. Chubby little fingers poke at my cheek before she turns her attention to my tangled hair. And I half-laugh, half-sob as a delighted squeal sounds before she wraps her hands around a section of hair and *pulls*.

She climbs right onto my lap in her determination, her entire focus on the hair in her grip, and I watch her through the tears that slip down my face as her own scrunches in pure concentration.

She's so... carefree. Unharmed. Safe. *Happy.*

Carefully, I lift my left hand and stroke it over her head, my fingers playing with her soft curls. Drinking her in.

We both pause at the sound of footsteps, and Alessia's hand moves to my shoulder as she looks around me, and I twist.

Dante. He's out of breath, his eyes settling on us as he comes to a stop on the other side of the hall. "I couldn't find—,"

His voice cuts off. And he doesn't move - doesn't even look like he's breathing as Alessia slides off my lap, her own gaze now pinned on the man who watches her with devastation clear to see on his face.

And as our daughter scoots across the hallway, Dante V'Arezzo falls to his knees.

I press my fist against my chest as if I can stop the stabbing pain that appears as Alessia crawls right up to her father with no fear in those green eyes. As if she *knows*.

And when she climbs into his lap, just as she did with me, Dante loosens a shuddering breath. Her hands land on his face, pushing his cheeks together as she regards him seriously.

They watch each other for long, silent seconds. I glance over as Luc descends the stairs, stopping short as he sees it too.

Alessia runs her palms over Dante's face, over and over again, feeling the stubble beneath her fingers with a fascinated expression. His lips twitch up into a smile as he watches her.

A MASTERY OF CROWS

And Alessia throws back her head and *laughs* - a pealing, joyous sound that rings out in the otherwise silent space, following it up with more of that incoherent babbling.

Dante nods as if he understands every word.

He doesn't move, except to lift up his hands so she can balance as she scrambles to her feet.

And his expression... is nothing I have ever seen.

Except, perhaps... when he looks at me.

"*Cuore mio*," he whispers finally, low and rough, before he glances at me with bright eyes. "My heart, Cat. She's perfect, *tentazione*."

She is perfect.

And this time, when he holds out his hand... I don't hesitate to take it.

~~G~~iovanni

My bare feet are near silent on the cool floor as I settle next to Luc. "Thanks for the clothes."

He flicks an inquisitive glance my way at my low murmur, nodding before turning back to them. I follow his gaze, my own chest clenching as Cat slowly moves across the floor to where Dante sits.

He looks... dazed. Unsteady, as he watches his daughter. Alessia has grown more since the photo was taken, another half-inch to the curls that bounce around her head as she uses the V'Arezzo capo like a climbing frame. She giggles as Cat settles back on her heels and watches them with a small smile as she pushes back the long sleeves of my sweatshirt.

Beside me, Luc rests his wrists on his bent knees with a smile. "That's a good sound, Fusco."

The sound of laughter. Of happiness. "Yes."

We both sit quietly, drinking it in for long minutes until Luc turns to me with a sigh. "It's not over."

"No." I don't take my eyes off them. "But we have bought ourselves a little time. Time we need, Luc."

Those who survived the extermination of the Asante compound will have carried the events straight to Matteo's ears. And Matteo has more men than Asante – *paid* men, mercenaries and assholes gathering like vermin who know nothing of the code of the Cosa Nostra. Those men only know the money that lines their pockets, without care or thought to our traditions.

"The Asante battle was a warm-up," I murmur. "We rest, regroup. Because the next one will be worse."

Luc looks grim when I glance at him. "I have plenty of information on him to share."

I dip my head. "Like I said. Rest first. You need it just as much as the rest of us, Morelli."

Perhaps more so. His cheekbones stand out in sharp prominence, his voice hardening. "He's a dead man."

I stay silent. I thought that, once. Thought that it would be as easy as a gunshot across a hotel reception to rid us of his filth.

Caterina paid the price for my mistake, then. Took a whip across her back to save my life.

My sister paid the price for my insolence before that.

I will not risk this family by rushing again. Matteo has taught me that, if nothing else.

"Soon," I say eventually. "But not yet."

"He has Amie," Luc says abruptly, and I cast him a sharp glance. "Cat's... friend. I couldn't have gotten Alessia away without her. She risked everything to stay behind. I can't... I can't leave her there."

There's pain there, and I understand his meaning. "Will he know? Matteo?"

And the guilt is almost visible as he swipes a hand over his face. "Yes. She was responsible for Alessia."

I follow his gaze to the little girl now demolishing one of the rugs as Dante watches with a delighted grin.

"We will already be too late to help her, Luc."

I keep my voice gentle, but he flinches nonetheless. "Maybe not."

Hope. It keeps all of us going in some way. Kept me going for those months that Cat was away from us, locked up with that asshole. So I nod. "Maybe not."

Amie is not the only person unaccounted for. I pull out my phone to check for updates, but the screen is empty. Nothing from Vincent or Tony, nothing to confirm that they found Frankie Costa in the aftermath of the battle.

Perhaps we could all do with a little more hope.

"A few days," I amend, looking at Luc. "And I'll help you find her."

"Find who?"

Luc stiffens as we both glance up. Cat lingers a few steps below, her eyes darting between us. "Who are you talking about?"

When Luc stays quiet, she crosses her arms. "*Luciano.*"

And despite her exhaustion, the ashy tinge to her golden skin... her tone is pure Corvo. Luc shifts, making space between us. "Come and sit down."

She eyes us both before settling into the spot, her body brushing against mine. I drink in the warmth of her as Luc explains.

Her skin has paled further when he finishes. "We're going to get her. Now."

"He'll be on high alert," I say the words quietly. "Matteo knows we'll be coming for him, Cat. He has more men than Asante did, and our side needs time to recover. He may even try to use her as a hostage."

"No," she breathes. There's horror there, in her face. "I know exactly what he's doing to her. I can't leave her alone there, Gio. Not when I know—,"

She stops abruptly, and Luc and I lock eyes over her head.

When I know what it feels like.

"She is not alone," I try again through the ache in my throat. "We *will* go for her, Cat. But we need to regain our strength. Rebuild our allies, pull in anyone that wasn't involved last time. Now that you're... back, it will be easier. We go now and *we will lose.*"

"Gio is right." Dante steps up in front of us, cradling Alessia as she nestles against his shoulder. He tears his eyes from her for a moment. "We have to be ready, Cat. It won't take long, but we will only get one chance."

He nods at me. "We cannot waste it."

She swings her gaze between us. "*Et tu, brutes?*"

But there's no heat there. She sighs, rubbing her hands over her face before she glances back up to Alessia. "I know you're right. But I still hate the idea of waiting."

"Not long," Luc murmurs. "And we have plenty to do in the meantime."

He gets to his feet. "Come with me. I'll find you rooms, and you can wash up before lunch."

All of us still when Alessia wriggles in Dante's arms. He's still holding her protectively, and his gaze moves to Luc when Alessia holds her arms out in demand.

Luc waits.

Dante sighs, then leans forward. "The women in my life have no taste."

No irritation lingers in his tone. Only a dry humor, as he holds her out.

"I disagree," Luc quips. He scoops up Alessia, bopping her nose. "Naturally. I'm going to be her favorite uncle, of course. Sorry, Fusco."

I look between the four of them, my eyebrows raising. Not something I'd particularly thought about, aside from getting her out of Matteo's reach. But my eyes narrow on Luc's smug expression, the competitiveness inside me rising. "We'll see."

Beside me, Cat shifts. I glance down to see her watching Alessia with a soft expression. But it shutters as she gets to her feet and makes her way upstairs. She doesn't look back.

Dante frowns, but I shake my head. "Give her some time to adjust."

He turns his scowl onto me instead. "I'm not pushing her. When did you turn into the *consigliere*?"

The reference to our most senior advisors within the Cosa Nostra makes me snort. "Perhaps we're all growing up, no?"

I don't wait for him to respond before I turn to follow Cat up the stairs. Luc is already there, pushing the door open to a bedroom a few doors down from mine. She ducks under his outstretched arm, and I slip into my own room.

I wait for a few moments, until footsteps echo outside my door as he heads back downstairs before slipping out again.

I don't knock.

Cat spins as I walk in, clutching the bloody remains of her dress to her chest. My sweatshirt is crumpled on the double bed beside her, the sound of the shower echoing out from the en-suite next to us. "Fucking *Christ*, Gio. Heard of knocking?"

My mouth feels dry as I stare at her, the words I hastily prepared locking up in my throat and refusing to come out.

She shifts, still covering herself even as she cocks an eyebrow at me. "Well?"

But her fingers tremble against the material.

I stay where I am. "I... missed you."

Brown eyes meet mine, creasing in the middle.

"Every single day," I continue. I don't move, keeping that distance between us. "Every day that you were gone, I *missed* you, Caterina Corvo."

"Gio." She whispers it, but I shake my head, holding my hand up in a silent plea.

"It was not so long ago that I thought I detested the sight of you. You were everywhere I looked, and it made my blood burn just to *look* at you."

The frown deepens, but I cut her off before she can speak.

"And then," I say softly, "I spent three months without you. Looking for you in every room, listening for your voice without even thinking about it, and I realized."

I'm close now. Close enough to pick out the tiny flecks of gold in her eyes as she looks up at me. "What did you realize?"

My voice lowers further. "That life without you is *cold*. Cold, and lonely, and hopeless. You took every bit of warmth in my life with you when you left, Corvo. I learned what it was to be without you, and I realized that I have no desire to exist in a world without you in it."

She inhales, and I glance down. To where she covers herself. And I brace.

"When you went back in...," I say quietly. Assessing the expression on her face. "He hurt you."

It's not a question. Because *this* Caterina – this Caterina is not the woman that walked away from me outside of the Asante compound.

There's a fragility to her now that threatens to undo me. And she confirms it as her eyes shutter. "I don't want to talk about it, Gio. Please."

Slowly, I nod, forcing that fury down until later. "Then I will not ask, not until you're ready. But I've been waiting for you for one hundred days, Caterina Corvo. And I don't want to go another day without holding you, but I will wait - unless you tell me I can."

The tense lines around her eyes smooth away, and she swallows. Her voice is barely audible when she speaks.

"Yes. Please."

That's all I need.

Caterina

Gio.

He moves with such fluid motion that it takes me by surprise as his arms wrap around me. Tight and secure as I sink into him, into the strength he offers, soaking in the warmth of his chest as I bury my face against it and breathe in the clean, citrus scent of the shower gel he must have used earlier.

I breathe him in as if I might absorb some of his strength at this moment, when I don't feel very strong at all. "I missed you too. Every day. I'm sorry... I'm sorry I left like that."

He shudders against me, and I wonder how much he has held back for my sake. How much it took to keep away in the hours since we found each other again, to organize everything we needed to get here as soon as possible, to step back and let the others fill the space he offered me while he made sure I was taken care of. "I should *never* have let you go back in there, Cat."

My hands, gripping the back of his shirt, twist. "Nobody *lets* me do anything, Gio Fusco. Haven't you learned that by now?"

He half-laughs, half-groans. "How did I come to love the most *infuriating* woman in the Cosa Nostra?"

My heart twists, squeezing inside my chest. And the words slip out, a hoarse whisper. "How did I get so lucky?"

He pulls back at that, pulls back so he can look into my face. His dark brows drop down into a true frown. "We will have to disagree on who is the lucky one."

Smiling, I bury my face back into him. And exhaustion tugs again, enough that the thought of the shower I desperately need becomes less appealing. "I need to... I have to shower. Stay with me?"

He tenses against me. "Are you sure?"

A black canopy.

A bare back.

"Yes," I force out. "But... keep your shirt on."

His tension doesn't abate at that. It grows, grows until he almost shakes against me. Gio's throat bobs, and then he steps back. "Of course."

Neither of us reference his clenched fists. And it doesn't help when I take a breath, backing up. Gio's eyes skate over me, and it's not desire that fills his face as he focuses on my upper right breastbone.

"I've seen it before," he says roughly when I open my mouth to explain. Rage darkens his eyes to near black, the blue almost invisible. "At the Cosa Nostra meeting."

My mouth closes with a snap. The meeting I was desperate to attend – to catch even a glimpse of them to keep me going, until Salvatore pulled out the vials he was so fond of and ripped even that small moment away from me. "I don't remember that."

"I know," he says, softer this time, although the line of his mouth remains tight. "Do you want to know what happened?"

I shake my head. "Stefan told me - after."

Gio pauses at that. "He gave me the information we needed to go in there and get you, you know."

My throat bobs. "He did?"

A nod. "He cares for you. And you... you went back in there for him, Cat."

"For Alessia," I correct. "But... yes. For him, too. I didn't want him to face the punishment Salvatore would have given for letting me go. I couldn't leave him there, Gio."

"I know," he says again. This time, he half-smiles. "I also know what it feels like to be on the receiving end of a Caterina Corvo rescue mission, remember. Asante never stood a chance against you."

"You don't mind, then?" I say the words lightly enough, but he considers them.

"No," he says finally. Those indigo blue eyes lock onto mine. "I find that I like this family you're building, Corvo. And I would very much like to be part of it. If you'll still have me."

"You already are," I breathe, stepping toward him. "I chose you, Gio Fusco."

I claimed him. Gio Fusco is *mine*.

And this time, I am the one who grips him. His hand runs over the back of my hair. "You should shower. Get some rest before lunch."

I release him only long enough to shuck off my underwear before taking his hand. And any fear I might have felt is wiped away as he keeps his eyes on my face, even as I lead him toward the bathroom. Gio leans against the doorway as I step into the shower, a watchful presence as the piping hot water cascades down my back.

Dark swirls of blood and soot wash away from me, swirling down the drain as I grab the shower gel without looking and wash.

Once.

Twice.

Again.

"Cat."

I scrub at the crook of my elbows as if I might be able to wash away the small needle marks that still dot my skin like purple freckles – that might always remain, if they haven't disappeared already. Yet another reminder.

My body is riddled with them.

Large hands close over mine, and I flinch away before I can stop it, my back hitting the white tiles.

Gio backs away, his hands raised even as he closes his eyes, his apology hoarse. "I'm sorry. God, Cat—,"

I reach out for him. "Wash my hair. Please."

And I force myself to turn, to close my eyes, not to flinch as he moves up behind me.

Not the same.

This is not the same.

"I'm fine," I say abruptly when I feel him hesitate. "*Please.*"

I cannot let myself fall apart.

Gio is careful not to touch my skin, his hands gentle as he massages in shampoo and uses the shower head to rinse it. Neither of us say anything as he shampoos it a second time. Then as he works in the conditioner, slowly combing through the tangled strands with his fingers.

It takes far, far longer than it needs to.

And neither of us mention my shuddering breaths. Or the tears that mix with the water that Gio brushes away with tender fingers.

He doesn't turn off the water until the shuddering stops. I lean against the wall, spent, as he collects a towel and wraps it around me. As he carefully dries my hair. We don't talk until I walk out of the bedroom and climb into the bed still wearing my towel, curling up. "Stay."

He sits facing the door, his back against the metal frame, and I use his legs as a pillow. Gio trails his fingers through my damp strands, teasing them out as my eyes start to close.

But I still don't sleep.

Stefano

I glance around the room again, noting the glittering blue of the Med in the distance from the shuttered window.

"Look, mamma." I keep my voice quiet. "You always loved the sea."

My mother doesn't respond. She stays where she is, curled up in the bed, and I wait for a few minutes before taking a light blue sheet from the end of the bed and draping it over her. "Some rest, then. It was a long trip. I'll bring some lunch up."

Iliana Asante only blinks, before her eyes close.

I walk out, my eyes scanning the corridor. Wondering which door belongs to Cat.

She has the others now.

She may not welcome me – not in the same way she did when we were forced together by circumstances. Perhaps Domenico Rossi was right to throw that accusation at me.

I will not hold her to it.

But I will stay, nonetheless. Until she tells me otherwise.

Movement down the hall, and I pause as someone slips out of a door, quietly pulling it closed.

Giovanni Fusco locks eyes with me as he turns, blue eyes flaring with surprise before he rocks back on his heels. He crosses his arms as I walk toward him. "Asan- Stefano."

"Gio." I turn my gaze to the door. "How is she?"

He frowns. "How did you know she was in there?"

My lips curve up. "Nobody is that careful about leaving an empty room. Unless you and V'Arezzo have a deeper relationship than I realized, I'm assuming it's Caterina."

He blinks. And then a low sound of amusement escapes him. "She's pretending to sleep, if you want to go in."

I frown at that, even as Gio steps away from the door to give me space, and I eye him in silent question as he slides his hands into the pockets of his chinos.

He lowers his voice further. "I know what it is to be the outsider. Caterina has always made her own choices, and I am grateful for it. I would be a hypocrite to argue with her now, no?"

My brows knit as the words filter through. I don't know the details of how Giovanni Fusco became part of... whatever this is, but I know enough. "*Il bacio della morte* – was it real?"

His face darkens. "Yes. Caterina is no fool, nor is she weak. She risked everything to keep my youngest sister safe despite my own actions, and I still live with those regrets. I likely always will."

My thoughts shift. Move to a room full of people, a bucket. The scent of her skin burning beneath my own hands. "How do you live with it?"

He studies me. "By trying to be a better man. She makes me *want* to be a better man." A half-smile. "If only to keep up with her."

I understand that, possibly more than he even realizes.

"Go on," he tilts his head toward the door. "Lunch will be ready soon. Morelli has a thing about family meals, you'll find."

Family meals.

"Thanks." It comes out gruffly, and Gio studies my face before he nods.

The door opens silently beneath my hand, and I slip into the room. The thin cotton curtains are pulled back, giving me another angle of the ocean outside as I cross to the bed. "Cat?"

I keep my voice low, just in case. But her brown eyes immediately blink open.

"You haven't slept," I say softly. She didn't sleep on the flight either, keeping her eyes closed but her body tense. "Why not?"

Her sigh is heavy, even as she shifts over in silent invitation. I climb onto the bed as she pulls herself up to sit beside me, her head leaning on my shoulder. I wait.

"Real?"

The quiet question threatens to shatter whatever pieces of my heart still remain. "*Real.*"

We sit in silence for a few moments.

"When I was under…," she whispers eventually. "I always dreamed, you know? Vivid, real dreams. Of all of them. Of you. Of a different life. It felt so real, Stefan, and then I would wake up. I - I know this is real. But if I go to sleep – what if it's not? What if I wake up and I'm still *there*?"

My breath catches. "You're not there anymore, Cat. It's over. He's dead."

She picks at a stray thread on the bedding. "Maybe. But he's still inside my head. Not so easy to kill there, as it turns out."

"Give it time," I say as gently as I can, even as the rage burns my throat. And the guilt. "It's been hours, Cat. Nobody expects you to walk away and forget it ever happened."

"I don't *have* time." Her voice raises a little, frustration leaking in. "Not when – there is so much to do, Stefan."

"Not right now." My voice firms. "We have a little time. Eat some food. Try to rest. Give yourself a break, Cat, and everything else will follow."

She makes an incredulous sound. "I couldn't even take my daggers when Gio offered them to me."

I nudge her. "You seem to have discovered a penchant for steak knives, however."

Her eyes glitter as she mock shoves me. "I need sharper ones. Not ones that bounce off people's heads."

But her face softens. "Real."

Instead of answering, I lift up her hand. Press it against my chest, so she can hear the thumping of my heart inside my chest. "You hear that?"

She nods, and I cup her cheek. "My heart only beats like that for you. *Ti amo*, Caterina."

And the weight in my chest lifts, when she whispers it back. "*Ti amo*, Stefan."

After a few minutes, I climb off the bed, and she glances up at me. "Where are you going?"

My eyebrow lifts. "I heard something about a family lunch? I wouldn't want to miss it."

She grins at me then, even if it's not as vibrant as it could be. "It's an experience."

"Well, then." I help her up, and she moves to the wardrobe in the corner. "I want all of the experiences with you, Caterina Corvo. We may as well start with lunch."

Caterina

Stefan's hand is tight around mine as we skirt around the piles of boxes in the entrance hall and walk into the bright, airy kitchen. The low murmur of conversation greets us, and I have to stop.

To take it in.

Luc is chopping something at the black granite counter, Gio leaning beside him with his arms crossed. Two beers sit on the counter beside them, icy cold droplets sliding down the glass bottles. Music is coming from somewhere, low and inviting.

And at the table—

Dante grins at me. "She's very clever, our *figlia*."

And he sounds so *proud* in that second that a lump appears in my throat. Slowly, I move my gaze to Alessia. She sits in his lap, her entire attention focused on the pasta heaped on the plate in front of her.

Every inch of space within two feet of her is *covered* in sauce.

Beside me, Stefano coughs in what sounds suspiciously like amusement.

Including Dante.

He doesn't seem to care that his pristine white shirt is splattered with sauce. Even his face and neck are covered, what looks like small fingerprints spread out on his cheeks. Instead, he watches as Alessia reaches for another piece of pasta, squishing it between her fingers.

Her own face is covered in orange sauce. Some of her curls stick out with it, and she burbles to herself before she shoves the entire piece of pasta in and chews it thoughtfully.

I take a step forward without thinking, but she swallows without hesitation.

Slowly, I make my way around the table. Dante follows my movements, his smile fading as I take a seat opposite them.

Avoiding his gaze, I keep my eyes on Alessia. Watch every movement she makes, as Dante returns to feeding her – or trying to.

A glass of wine appears in front of me, and I look up at Luc. He still looks exhausted, but he offers me a smile as he passes a beer to Stefano. "I ordered some supplies. Including clothes. They're in the hall."

I glance down at the white shirt I'm wearing as a dress. "Thanks."

His hand brushes against my shoulder before he returns to the meal. I glance to the door as Gio slides into the seat beside mine, watching Dante and Alessia. "Has anyone seen Dom?"

Heads shake.

"He's in his room," Luc says, tipping back his beer and taking a deep swig. "I'll put some food aside if he doesn't come down. For your mother too. She's not coming down?"

Stefano jerks at the question Luc aims at him. "No. She... prefers the quiet. *Grazie.*"

My eyes slide back to Alessia. I watch her play with the pasta, with Dante's watch. Her own eyes, bright green with vivid curiosity, move around the room.

They settle on me. And she starts to wriggle against Dante's hold, her hands out.

I watch with my heart in my mouth as she slides from his lap, her hand wrapped around his finger as she uses the edge of the table to steady herself. And then she starts to move, determination in every wobbling step as she circles the round table, her finger slipping from Dante's as he settles back into his seat and crosses his arms.

His eyebrow raises when I glare at him. Challenging.

Alessia rounds the square wooden table, and my arm flies out when she wobbles. She grips it with a toothy grin, pulling on it as she moves closer. And my heart... it squeezes, twists, as she reaches the edge of my chair and holds out her arm.

My daughter is a surprisingly heavy bundle in my arms as I carefully lift her. Sticky fingers immediately tangle in my hair, a hand on my cheek as she leans in close.

My throat bobs.

She settles against me, playing with damp strands of hair as Luc places steaming plates of pasta down. All of them try hard not to stare as I fumble my way around Alessia, pausing to offer her a piece of pasta that she accepts after scrutinizing it.

"Does she... what does she have? Need?" I ask awkwardly.

Useless.

Bea would have known what she needed.

Luc waves his hand. A hint of color appears on his cheeks. "I may have gotten a little carried away. But I thought if she stays, she'll need—,"

I straighten. "Stays?"

Dante straightens as well. "She won't be able to come with us, Cat. Not until this is over."

My hands slip around her, holding her. "Who?"

"My mother." Luc taps his fingers against the table. "She'll be back in a few days. She'd be delighted to have a little one around the house, Caterina. The staff will help."

I stiffen, irritation curling through me. "Then it's settled, it seems."

And I hate myself, as Luc flinches. "I'm sorry. That wasn't – it's only a suggestion. If there's anything else you want to do—,"

But there isn't.

I should have thought about it. But I *didn't*.

Pull yourself together, Corvo.

I breathe in the sweet, soapy, tinged-with-tomato scent that lingers in her hair as she reaches for more pasta.

"No," I say quietly. "I'm sorry. You're right. Of course she can't come."

Another separation beckons, for who knows how long.

I wonder if I'll come back, this time. If I'll ever have that time with her, to learn from her, to learn how to be what she needs.

Alessia holds up some pasta to my mouth, and I snap my teeth at it. My hand jumps up to catch the back of her head as she throws it back, a loud, happy cackle of laughter before she offers it to me again. And my lips curve up, as I force that sadness down.

I will come back, I promise her silently. *I'll come back for you.*

Her eyes move past me and stop. I turn to see Stefano watching. He stares at Alessia, and she stares back at him. "Ba."

He freezes when she leans forward. Her hands open and close in a clear demand. "*Ba!*"

"I think she wants you." I bite my lip to hide my smile as he stiffens.

"I don't...," he clears his throat. "I've never held a baby."

But he reaches out for her, and she says it again as he lifts her, settling her against his large chest. His hand is large enough to cover her entire back as she buries her face into his shirt, smearing sauce over it. A small yawn sounds. "Ba."

Dante frowns. "Like I said. No taste."

I scowl at him, but he looks unrepentant. Across from me, Gio smirks. "What did you say about being the... what was it... *favorite uncle*, Morelli?"

Luc narrows his eyes. "Eighteen years is a long time, *Fusco*. She'll come back to me. Won't you, *cuoricino*?"

Stefano's voice is a low, uncertain rumble. "She's...ah, asleep."

My eyes slide over them all. At Stefano, with Alessia curled up against his chest. At Gio and Luc as they rib each other. And at Dante, who glances at the door before looking back to me. "Go. We've got her. Or... Asante has, it seems."

Slowly, I push my chair back. "Gio... where are my knives?"

One of us is missing, and I'm not going to let him hide away.

Domenico

I flex my hands again. Glance down at the array of scars that cover my knuckles in layers of broken, battered skin. Some are older. And some... some are more recent.

One deep red gouge opens up as the skin stretches, a bead of blood trailing down my hand. It looks almost black in the cool darkness of the room, the curtains pulled shut to block out the warmth of the sun.

As I'm trying to block out... everything.

The knock on the door has my head jerking up. Ignoring it, I wait for them to leave. But it only comes again.

Again. Louder this time.

Her voice rings out. "I'm not going anywhere, Domenico Rossi. Answer the fucking door."

I purse my lips. Wait her out. The door is locked.

My brows dip down at the scraping sound. Then the bang. Several of them, one after the other.

And my door... opens. Splinters of wood rain down against the floor.

Cat stalks inside, meeting my glare with one of her own. "Why are you on the floor?"

My jaw clenches as I take in the knife she twirls between her fingers. "Heard of privacy?"

"You *never* want privacy." Her eyes travel over me. Over my bare, battered skin, the towel around my waist as I sit on the floor against the wall. "Not from me."

I stiffen as she pauses in front of me. "Cat – just leave me alone."

She doesn't leave. She drops to her knees instead, her eyes running over my body, and I inhale sharply as her fingers reach out and brush against one of the bruises on my neck. She doesn't say anything, only tracing the shape before she moves on to the next.

The next.

And the next, her lips moving although I can't hear the words.

I stay silent, watching her.

"Thirty-seven," she whispers finally. "What did he do to you?"

"This wasn't him." She turns her face to mine scanning my expression. "I got these from the ring."

Cat only shakes her head, lips thinning. "Maybe, but it *was* him. He made you fight."

"And I made him a lot of money." My tone is caustic. "His favorite lapdog. I never lost a fight."

Buzzing in my veins.

Blood, spilling across the floor.

When she reaches for me again, my hand snaps out to grip her wrist, and I snarl. "*Don't.*"

"You think I'm scared of you, Domenico?" She glares right back at me, her hair falling around her face.

"I don't know how many people I killed."

Cat pauses.

"I don't *know*." I look down again, rub the bead of blood into my skin. "A lot. Dozens, maybe. Anyone he wanted to get rid of. The young, the old – most of them I can't even fucking *remember*. He put them in with me, and I finished them, Cat. There's so much fucking blood on my hands that they will never be clean. *Don't touch me*."

She pulls her hand away, but only to take me in properly. The redness of my skin. "How many showers have you had?"

I lift my eyes to hers, my voice hoarse. "Not enough."

Not nearly enough. I feel coated in shame, oily and covered in the filth of the last few months.

Her hand rises to my cheek, and this time, she ignores my attempts to pull away. She grips my face between her hands, her forehead pressing against mine. "Listen to me."

"*Please—*,"

"*No*," she breathes. "You damn well listen to me, Domenico Rossi. You are not Matteo's creature. He does not own you. You are mine, you understand? You are mine, and I am yours. And we are *endgame*, you and I. You told me that once, and I have held onto it, Dom. I held onto it every fucking day that we were apart, and I will not let him keep us apart for another fucking day. They do not get to stay inside our heads and ruin us."

Her grip tightens. "Whatever you did because of him – own it. He used you as a weapon, Dom, and you didn't have a choice, but now you do. Recognise it. You feel guilty? Ashamed? Join the club because there is plenty of fucking room. But you do not get to block *me* out, and let *him* in."

Both of us are breathing heavily. I don't close my eyes, don't look away from her, our noses brushing against each other. "It's still there. That anger. It wants *out*, Cat, and I don't want to be anywhere near you – near any of you - when it happens."

And she shakes me. "You are the one person who has always had faith in me, Dom. Don't lose it now. I am strong enough to help you fight your battles, and you are strong enough to help me fight mine."

I take a ragged breath. Another. "Together."

"Always," she breathes. "Besides. You owe me a trip to the beach and a dance at sunset. I haven't forgotten."

I lift my hand, brushing it against her cheek. "You weren't awake for that conversation."

"I have my sources." She stands, holding out her hand. "Get up, Domenico. Consider it an order if you need to. If I'm still your capo."

Always.

When I'm up, she directs me to the bed. "You look worse than I do. Get some sleep."

I resist. "Not without you."

Something about her presence... it chases those shadows away. Still there but lingering at a distance instead of smothering me with darkness.

We lay facing each other. I examine her face as though it's the first time, and she does the same to me.

Both of us changed beyond recognition. And yet... not, at the same time.

We're still here. Still Caterina Corvo, and Domenico Rossi.

"You are my endgame," I murmur. "Always, Cat."

CATERINA

I wake up with a gasp.

The room is dark, the low buzz of an air conditioning unit the only noise as I stare at the ceiling. My chest lifts up and down as if I've been running.

Not there.

I'm not there.

Swallowing, I scrunch my eyes closed and force out a breath before I turn to my right.

My body goes rigid.

Not the same.

This is not the same.

But I can't look away from the bare expanse of skin that greets me.

A black canopy.

A bare back.

The noise that slips from my lips sounds more animal than human. Nausea surges, and I scramble off the bed, backing up until I hit the wall and slide down.

On the bed, Dom shifts, his hand reaching out to the empty space as he turns to face my direction. I hold my breath, waiting until he settles.

He doesn't need my nightmares to add to his own. Not tonight.

My head thumps against the wall as I look to the window. I slept for a few hours, at least – more than I've slept since we left for Sicily, the darkness outside telling me that we probably missed dinner.

I fight my own breathing, fight to calm down, but the dizziness in my head only grows until I'm shaking.

I need air.

I stumble for the door, only stopping to scoop my daggers off the floor before darting blindly down the hall.

The world outside is silent in that way that you can only hear at night. The witching hour, some call it. I invade that quiet space, my breathing ragged and harsh as I head outside. The warmth of the Italian air kisses my face, brushes away the stickiness of those panicked minutes as the nausea clutching my stomach begins to recede.

I take a few more steps out into the courtyard, looking around at the view that stretches for miles in front of me.

The ocean greets me on one side, dark and glittering beneath the few stars that dot the clear night sky. On the other, rows of trees stretch as far as my eyes can see, perfectly planted in patterns and blooming with the small white flowers that will eventually turn to olives, ready to be harvested late in the autumn.

I start walking in that direction, gripping my knives tightly as I weave in and out, losing myself in the familiar dry, woody scent. It smells like memories – like long, hot summers spent running through the groves at our own estate, several hours to the South in Ragusa.

A lifetime ago.

I start to pick up speed, my feet padding against the hard ground until I'm running, flying over twigs and leaves that scratch the soles of my feet. I race through the grove, zigzagging between lines of trees until I have to stop, my lungs screaming for air.

I wait only as long as I need to before I take off again, my hair catching on low-hanging branches. My energy is sapped far too soon, and I slow to a walk, panting.

The trees rustle, and my hand tightens around my knives. Slowly, I slide one into my palm.

I spin, my arm shooting out, and the edge of my dagger *barely* misses Luc's face as he slips out of reach as smoothly as he used to on the practice mats.

I yank it back, breathing heavily. "*Testa di cazzo*, Luciano. I could have killed you! What are you even doing out here?"

He only slips his hands into his pockets, looking utterly unconcerned. But his eyes glitter. "Hardly. You're out of practice, little crow. And you set off every security measure around the villa with your little evening run."

Irritated at the truth in his words, I turn my back on him. "I'll be back soon."

"Spar with me."

Turning slowly, I glare at him. "What?"

He gestures to the space around us. "You and me. Like old times. Right here."

I scoff, but something flickers in my chest. "It's the middle of the night, Luc."

He only steps closer, his voice a low murmur as he lifts my hair in his hand, winding it around his finger before letting it slip away. "So? You're here. I'm here. And you seem to have some excess energy to burn."

He pauses. "Unless you want to do something *else,* of course. I'm equally happy with either."

There's no heat in his words. His gaze sweeps over me, assessing. Searching. And his lips tighten at whatever expression crosses my face.

Luciano Morelli doesn't miss a thing.

"Sparring it is, then," he says – a little too gently. "Or we could talk about whatever sent you flying out here as if the hounds of hell were snapping at your heels."

I toss him a dagger instead, and he snatches it from mid-air.

Show off.

I spring, but he's ready, pushing me back and going for a low sweep that I can see a mile away. Sliding out, I give him a filthy look. "Don't take it easy on me."

"I happen to like you in one piece." He easily dodges the flurry of movement, the slash of knives as he dances back. "And whatever you tell yourself, you need the practice."

"Ass." I launch myself at that, speeding up until our knives smash together with a metallic clang. He only smirks, our faces a few inches together.

"Fucking hell," he whispers. "I've missed fighting with you, Caterina."

His words send my stomach flipping, but I push him back anyway. "Flattery will still get you on your back."

He wiggles his eyebrows. "Promise?"

And the laugh bubbles up my throat before I can stop it. "At least dance with me first."

He more than meets my challenge. We move up and down the path as I try to catch him. But... he's right. I am out of practice.

He slips beneath my guard, and I pause as his hand slips around my throat. "My win, I believe. In a real fight, you'd be dead."

I swallow as his breath heats my neck. And his lips brush against my exposed skin, the shirt I'm wearing oversized enough to give him easy access. "*Luc.*"

Heat. So much heat, as his palms rest on my shoulder. Slowly, he draws them down my arms, pressing against my back.

I let myself relax into him as he lifts my right hand. "Your guard is too high here."

I nod wordlessly, inhaling as his hand slips to my stomach. "And this arm – it's too tense. Keep it more relaxed, and you'll have more fluidity."

"Back to basics," I whisper.

He turns me then, my body shifting against his. "We all have to go back to basics sometimes, little crow."

I stare up at him. "You weren't sleeping either, were you?"

Silently, he shakes his head.

I take his hand in mine, lift it to my face. The scarring remains, a permanent memory of the night he dug me out of the ground. "You never gave up."

I'm not talking about that, and he knows it. His throat bobs. "I keep my promises."

He doesn't move as my hands slip to his shirt, and I push it up. My throat closes up at the sight of the two vivid red scars. "I thought—,"

Hands close over mine. Cover up those scars, those memories of him on the ground, crawling toward me, toward Alessia.

"It will take more than a little cut," Luc says softly, "to take me away from you, Caterina."

The dampness in my eyes spills over onto my cheeks. "You never gave up. You got her out."

I cup his cheeks when he tries to look away. "I had help, in the end."

Amie. He walked away, leaving her there to save Alessia.

The guilt is plastered over his face, and I swallow down that sudden, irrational fear.

I know how it feels to be locked in an impossible situation. How easily feelings can develop. And even the thought of it feels unbearable, the thought of losing him in that way—

I suck in a breath to ask, but warm lips cover mine. Luc kisses me gently, reverently, before he pulls back, reading my mind as he always has. "No. There is only one woman I love, and she's standing in front of me right now."

"Luc—."

"I love *you*," he says fiercely. "And I will keep loving you. On all of your good days, your bad days, and every day in between. I love your shadows and your lines and every single fucking part of you, little crow."

He brushes my tears away. "Every single piece of this jagged heart of mine is yours."

And then he grins at me. "My condolences."

I choke out a laugh, and then his lips are on mine again. There is nothing invasive about his touch – it's almost inquisitive. A gentle question, rather than a forceful push.

I'm the one who pushes. I kiss him back, softly at first, relishing in the feel of him against me as my hands slip to his face and I pull him closer, my arm winding around his neck. Luc's arms slip around my back, fingers wrapping into my tangled hair, and I push him back, blindly searching until his back hits the closest tree.

When I tear my lips away, pressing them to his cheek – lower – his hands grip my hips. "Cat. We don't have to—,"

My voice is firm. "He does not get to take this from us."

This connection, this sensation—

They have already taken too much.

No more.

Luc's grip tightens at my words. He opens his mouth, but I slam my lips against his, my fingers moving to the buttons on his shirt before I pull back to take a breath. "Keep this on?"

He only nods, his eyes following the path of my fingers as I flick the buttons open on my own shirt and shrug it off, letting it fall to the ground.

He says nothing, as I stand there, bared before him under the stars. His hazel gaze sweeps over me, lingers on the white scar marring my breastbone.

My hand raises instinctively but he catches it. "We all have scars. Yours are part of your story, Cat. Every part of you is beautiful to me."

He traces his fingers over it, follows the trail with his lips as I sink into him. He swaps our positions, nudging me back against the tree as his lips move lower.

Lower.

His hands wrap around my thighs as he lifts me up, my legs hooking over his shoulders. I'm already wet, trembling with need as he brushes his lips against my pussy. And my hands tangle in his hair, holding him against me, my mouth opening in a silent cry as he swipes his tongue against my center.

Once, twice. Again, and again. He flicks over my clit in rapid motions, his teeth grazing over the sensitive nub and his hands sinking into my hips, holding me still.

Our breathing is the only sound, the small, trembling noises he pulls from me the melody he works with as he devours me. "Luc, I want—,"

My words cut off, body convulsing, as he gently bites down around my clit.

"*You*. Now."

He pulls his head back, his lips and chin shining. His eyes glitter at me. "I haven't tasted you in months. I'm not nearly done."

It takes more effort than I have in my shaking body to push against him. To push him down, until he's laying on his back and I'm crawling over him, flicking open the buttons on his pants as he lifts his hips and I pull them off.

I run my fingers up the underside of his velvet shaft, already solid and heavy, and he hisses as I play with the metal rungs lining his cock. "This will be over very quickly if you keep doing that, little crow."

I run my tongue over the head of his cock, leisurely tasting him as his hips buck and he swears. "Patience is a virtue, Luciano."

But it's been *months*. Months without him, without this. So I don't tease any more, shifting my hips up until I'm hovering over him, my pussy brushing against his head with excruciating sensitivity as I sink down – inch by inch, thick and hard, pushing up and filling me until I have to rock my hips to get him deeper.

He watches every movement, his eyes on my face as I throw my head back on a moan and he bottoms out inside me. His fingers dig into my hips, holding me in place. "Wait."

Panting, I glance down at him. His hands run up my thighs, brush my aching nipples, and I lean forward to capture his lips before starting to rock.

Our breathing mingles, hot and damp as we move together in fluid motion, my hips rolling over him. Luc touches me everywhere – my shoulders, my breasts, my stomach – touches me as if reminding me where I am.

I do not forget.

His fingers find my clit, plucking and flicking, and my release rushes upon me almost by surprise as my back bows and I clench on him.

Luc follows me over the edge with my name on his lips and his hips pushing up, filling me with heat and *him*.

We use my shirt to clean up, before he lays back on the cool ground and I lay down on *him*. We lay quietly, both of us looking up at the sky.

He doesn't say anything. He just... waits.

And the words come. Quietly, at first. And then more – until I'm almost tripping over them, his hand stroking up and down my back, wiping my face when the memories become too much.

And when I'm done, the energy leaching from my body, Luc only holds me closer. He presses my palm against his chest so I can feel his heartbeat.

Real.

And slowly, I drift off into sleep.

Dante

"*Merda.*"

I stare down at Alessia in despair. "For such a small child... you make a *lot* of mess."

She kicks her feet, and I catch one, balancing her. I glance around the room, hoping for divine intervention.

Of all the thoughts that overtook my mind these last few months... diaper changing was *not* one of them.

I stare down at my daughter, and then over to the bed, where the diaper bag sits. I suddenly understand the shit-eating grin Luc was wearing when he passed it to me last night.

The three feet between us may as well be a mile.

Alessia kicks her feet again, her face scrunching up as I try not to panic. Balancing her with one hand, I stretch out for the bag, swearing under my breath. Not even close.

"Need some help?"

Stiffening, I glance over my shoulder at Gio. He leans against the doorframe, clearly trying not to laugh. "Do not."

He holds up his hands. "Fine. No help needed."

"*Wait—*,"

The smirk on his face as he strolls in and lifts the bag from the bed wipes away as he gets closer. "Fucking hell."

"Yeah." We both stare down at Alessia. "Do you know how to do this?"

"It can't be that hard." He frowns.

It can, in fact, be that fucking hard.

I drop another wipe into the trash with a wince. I'm only glad Rocco can't see me. Next to me, Gio unsuccessfully tries to hide his gag. "Remind me why I'm helping you with this, V'Arezzo."

"Leave, and I will fucking shoot you." We wrangle the diaper beneath Alessia, battling with the ridiculous number of tabs on display until they're all stuck to... something, at least.

"There." I hoist her up triumphantly. "Nice and clean, *il mio cuore*."

The smile slips off my face as quickly as the diaper slips to the floor. "What the *fu—*,"

The second time proves more successful, and Gio hands me a playsuit with approximately one hundred fucking buttons. I stare down at it. "Tell me there's a two-piece in there. A dress. Anything but the damn playsuit."

He holds up a sundress instead, and I force the relief from my face as I pull it over her head. Alessia claps her hands. "Ma."

Gio and I exchange glances as she says it again.

"Where is she?" he asks quietly, and I lift up my shoulder as I balance Alessia with one hand.

"Not here." I know. I went looking for her this morning. "With Luc, I think."

"She's scared." He says the words quietly, his gaze on Alessia. "She's scared that if she gets too close, that it will all be taken from her again."

"I know that."

None of us know how much time we'll have. Life in the Cosa Nostra does not lend itself to a happy retirement.

All the more reason to live day by day. I stroke my hand down Alessia's back. "She is a gift, Gio."

"Family," he says quietly.

I shoot him a look. "Have you heard anything from yours? You have an estate here too, right?"

He nods. "My parents are an hour away to the South. With Rosa there... I need to go and visit them."

He looks heavy at the thought. I consider my last sighting of Carlos Fusco. He lost his daughter in the most horrific way.

And now... the bottom drops out of my stomach as I think of it.

"I've never seen that area. Mind if I tag along? Unless you'd prefer to go alone."

He glances at me, surprise making his brows lift. "No. I would... it's a nice area."

I clear my throat. "Then it's settled."

We walk downstairs into the kitchen, greeted by the sight of Stefano Asante. He sits with a coffee in front of him, dark eyes raising above the top of the newspaper in his hands. "Good morning."

I offer him a nod. My *daughter*, however – who I have decided will need to be watched with an eagle eye as she grows older – lets out a sound of pure excitement, throwing herself forward with such enthusiasm that I nearly lose hold of her. "*Ba!*"

Stefano puts down the paper, a wary look on his face as he glances between us. "Uh. Should I...,"

Sighing, I stalk toward him. Alessia throws herself into his arms, patting his face as I head for the coffee.

"I don't get a *Ba*," I mutter in irritation as I grab a cup. "Not even a *Da*."

But Stefano fucking Asante is her favorite person.

A thought strikes me, and I spin, pointing the spoon at him. "Can you change a diaper?"

He blinks at the demand in my tone. Dark brows knit together. "No."

I take a breath. A deep one.

Gio pulls containers out of the refrigerator, frowning as he examines the contents. He piles them high on the table as I pull one toward me. He offers me a plate and a knife. "For the fruit."

Nodding, I start cutting things up before I slide the plate over to Stefano. Alessia settles on his lap with a fistful of strawberry, and I get up to fill her drinking cup with water.

"Well, isn't this very domesticated." Luc strolls into the kitchen, and I straighten as Cat follows behind him.

She's changed into loose, flowing white trousers and a deep red blouse. With her hair scraped back into a high ponytail, she looks – like *herself*.

More comfortable, somehow.

She offers me a small smile as she slips into a seat, her eyes immediately traveling to Alessia. I note the way she watches her, the way her eyes soften.

And the way she pulls her gaze away. Instead, she places a phone on the table. "I need everyone's numbers. Vincent. Tony—."

"I have them." We all turn at the low rumble. Domenico surveys the set-up with lowered brows, and I point to an empty seat in silent invitation. He turns back to Cat as he sits. "I know them, I mean."

I half-watch as he reels off numbers by memory and Cat types them in, nodding in thanks before she sits back.

Luc places a fresh coffee beside her as she looks up. "We need to start planning. Today."

Again, her eyes linger on Alessia, and move away.

"Matteo won't wait," she continues, her voice tight. "And I've had enough of him leading us around by the damn nose."

I survey her, my fist clenching on the table. "You need to rest."

"I need to kill him," she snaps back at me. "The longer we wait, the stronger he'll get. *He knows we're coming.* The more we put it off, the more fucking time he has to plan something to fuck us all over. I'm done with waiting."

"So what?" Gio crosses his arms. "Do you have a plan?"

"Preferably one that doesn't involve you going off and sacrificing yourself for the rest of us." My caustic words make her flinch. But I mean it, as I meet her glare with one of my own. "If I even think you're planning some hero shit, *tentazione*, I'll tie you down myself."

Her cheeks flood with color. "Fuck you, Dante."

"You already did," I snap, throwing my hand out. "But you won't even look at the consequences."

Shit – *shit*.

The whole table falls silent. The color drains from Cat's face. And regret tightens my throat, even as Dom jumps up from his seat, his face darkening with fury and his fists clenching. "The *fuck* did you just say?"

"Steady—,"

"Fucking *Christ*, Dante—,"

I ignore them. All of them, pinning my eyes on her.

"*Ti amo*," I breathe. "I'm sorry. *Ti amo*, Caterina Corvo. I love you. Always. But you promised me that we would face this together."

And those walls of hers feel higher than ever.

"If you walk into this fight," I push the words out around the fear that holds my heart in a vice grip, "thinking that you will not walk back out, then you won't come home, Cat. I need you to believe that you can *win*."

She takes a breath. Her hands clench on the wooden table. "That's not true. I don't think that."

She's not convincing anyone. Least of all me.

"Then why are you keeping away from her?" My heart twists, shreds inside my chest. "Everything you have given, and bartered, and sacrificed – all to keep her safe, to get to this point. And now she is here, and we will never get *this* time again. There will be more days – but these first, precious days will be *gone*, Cat. Don't waste them. *Please*."

My breath locks inside my chest as I stare at her. "When will you stop believing that your life is worth the least?"

I have no intention of letting her die in this battle. And Matteo Corvo will not leave it alive. I can feel it, like a knowing in my chest.

He will not live for what he has done to them. Even if it takes my own life to see it through.

"When we walk out there," I say finally. Heavily. "These are the days I will hold close, *tentazione*. A reminder of what we are fighting for."

I stand. I need some fucking air.

Cat is still in her chair, her face ashen as I move past her, stopping.

"You let the bad memories take over, we've already lost."

Caterina

Silence.

My hands are still gripping the table. I force myself to release them, to look up.

Stefano meets my eyes, his own soft. There's too much understanding there, so I look down. Alessia looks unfazed by our harsh words, still picking at strawberries as Stefan cradles her.

I hate him. Hate him for being so fucking unsufferable, overbearing... and *right*.

Nobody stops me as I shove my chair back and walk out.

When will you stop believing that your life is worth the least?

Instead of going outside, I make my way upstairs, pausing outside a door.

I don't knock. But I gently open it, and step inside.

Iliana Asante turns her head toward me. She doesn't say anything as I lean back against the door. "*Buongiorno, signora.*"

When nothing happens, I pad further into the room. A chair has been set up next to the window, the curtains open and blowing gently in the breeze. Iliana turns her face back to it, her eyes closing.

Slowly, I settle down onto the floor next to her. We sit in silence for long minutes, peaceful silence. There are no expectations here. And the weight in my chest, the heaviness caused by Dante's words, begins to lessen.

"I don't know what to do," I say into the quiet room. Iliana says nothing, her eyes still closed.

I cannot lose them.

I cannot lose anyone else.

And Dante – he was right, but he was wrong, too.

I don't want to die. Don't intend to. I will fight with every last breath left in my body to come home to them.

But if the choice is between me or them, then there will be no choice at all.

"Is it so bad?" I wonder aloud. "To love them more than I love myself? Isn't that what love is supposed to be?"

I never expected this. Never expected to find *this* – these men, this family that I would give everything for.

And my daughter.

"I will not give her another mother to lose," I whisper. My vision blurs.

I let my head rest against the side of Iliana's chair and close my eyes. The only sound is my hitched breathing.

And it stops altogether, as a hand gently strokes across the top of my head. My eyes fly open, my mouth falling open before I close it. Unwilling to do anything that might make Iliana panic, that might throw her back into that still, silent state.

So we sit. And all the while, Stefan's mother strokes my hair.

Comforting, as my tears flow freely.

Time slowly ticks away before the door opens again. Iliana's fingers slip away from my hair as Stefan ducks in, a tray in his hands.

I offer him a half-smile. "Your mother is a good listener."

His own lips lift, but his eyes are sad as he sets the tray down on a table close to us, leaning in to kiss Iliana's cheek. "She is. *Buongiorno,* mamma."

His hand cups my cheek, his thumb tracing my cheekbone. "V'Arezzo is an ass. But he loves you."

I frown at him. "I need someone on my side here."

He smiles at that. "I'll always be on your side."

I humph, but take his outstretched hand, letting him help me to my feet and stretching out my numb legs. "I know he does. And... he wasn't wrong."

"I know that too," Stefan says quietly. "No time spent loving someone is ever wasted, Cat. And I see your face when you watch her. You *want* to be closer. If it was something else holding you back, that would be different. But you both *deserve* to have this time with each other."

I slide my gaze to him. "He sent you in here, didn't he?"

Stefan shakes his head. "He hasn't come back."

Twisting in my chest. "I'll... I'll think about it."

Consider if the pain of being ripped from Alessia again is something I can take. Something I can put her through.

I wait as Stefan pulls the tray close to his mother. Her eyes flicker in my direction, just once. But she says nothing as we leave, and Stefan sighs. "She's adjusting well, at least."

I clear my throat. "Does she ever... instigate contact? Touch?"

He gives me a strange look. "Not that I can remember. Why?"

I stop in the middle of the hall. "She...I mean, it sounds strange, but... she stroked my hair. I was upset when I went in, and she just did it." He stops a foot or so ahead of me, turning. "I'm sorry—,"

Stefan holds up his hand, his eyes bright. "*Don't*. Don't apologize. You're sure?"

I nod, my stomach flipping at the hope in his face. "She stopped, though."

"Doesn't matter," he breathes. "This is... it's a good day, Cat."

I slip my hand into his, squeeze it as we make our way back downstairs. "Good. What are you doing now? Because I could use a sparring partner. I just need to make a call."

We've sparred together over the years, but not often. He nods. "Luc has a gym. Meet you down there?"

He brushes his lips against mine at the door before he withdraws. "I haven't thanked you yet, I realized earlier."

"What for?"

"This." He waves his hand around us, taking in the empty hall. "I didn't think I would ever get out of there, Cat. I thought I would stay in that hellhole for the rest of my life – until he decided I wasn't worth keeping alive anymore."

"Stefan," I whisper, but he shakes his head.

"And then you came," he continues. "With your fire, and your steak knife—" I punch his shoulder, and he laughs, low and rough, "—and as much as I wish you had never been there... I am more than grateful to be here, Caterina Corvo. With you."

I don't have any words. Don't want to imagine him still there, a hostage under Salvatore's control. So instead, I rise up, pressing my lips to his. "I claimed you. You're mine."

His lips curl beneath mine. "Yes."

After he leaves to change, I duck into the bedroom and pull out my new phone, pressing it to my ear as it rings out.

"Sì."

My shoulders loosen at the guarded voice that answers. "Vincent. It's me."

A pause, and then a relieved inhale. "I'm so fucking glad to hear your voice. How are you doing?"

"Fine." I pause. "Better. How are you?"

He snorts. "The bullet barely grazed me. Up and walking around."

"Take it easy. Please. How are things there?"

I take a seat on the bed, my frown deepening as he speaks. "They're still on campus?"

Vincent makes a noise of affirmation. "I think we should pull everyone out, Cat. Matteo's men aren't fucking around. He's angry."

I think it over, tapping my fingers against my knee. "Not angry. *Scared*. He wants us spread out, Vincent. The further apart we are, the harder it is to organize. Matteo knows the campus is a key location for us. Keeping his men stationed there is just a reminder."

And if I walk through those gates, their guns will not hesitate to point in my direction. "I won't abandon it. Keep your head down. Tell the others – I won't be long. If anyone does want to leave... let them. I won't force anyone to stay. Tell them that too."

Even though I need every soldier I have, every scrap of manpower I can gather. I can't afford to lose any.

Vincent clearly knows it too. "Cat...,"

"Forcing them to stay would make me tantamount to Matteo, Vincent." I study the floor, turning the thoughts over in my mind. "Our people are not machines to die for us at will. That's not what the hierarchy is for."

We care for those under us – or we used to. I cannot – will not - force anyone to die for me. Honor, loyalty – *those* are the traits of the Cosa Nostra. Something Matteo has twisted and warped in his push for power.

"And Matteo?" Vincent sounds subdued. "He's gathering more men. Hundreds."

My lips curve up at that. "I'm working on it. Can you send me Alessandro's number?"

We talk for a few minutes longer, before I broach the topic lingering in my mind. "Any news on Frankie? Tony?"

"Nothing." Vincent's anger is clear. "She's vanished, Cat. Tony – he blames himself for letting her go. He's still searching, doesn't stop to sleep, but it doesn't look good."

My eyes close. "If you hear *anything*, I want to know straight away. Do you need anything else from me?"

"A miracle would be nice." There's humor there, but he sounds tired.

"It won't be long now. The end is coming."

I just don't know who will be left standing.

~~G~~IOVANNI

I adjust the strap on my watch as I jog down the steps into the entrance hall. Ahead of me, Cat turns, her brows flicking upward as she takes in my shirt, the smart trousers. After a murmur into the phone she's holding, she ends the call. "Where are you going?"

I hesitate. "To see my parents. The estate isn't far."

The hint of a smile slides away from her face. "Of course. How are they?"

I shrug. Truthfully, I have no idea how to answer that question. And shame fills me at the thought of it. I have been distant these last few months. Unable to focus on something that no matter what I do, I cannot *fix*.

I will never be able to bring Nicci back. That's the only thing they want from me, and it's something I cannot give them.

A brush against my arm. "Gio?"

I jerk. "I... sorry. It's not going to be a pleasant trip."

Her frown deepens. "I can come with you. Although... do they know?"

About her.

"No," I breathe. "They're past the point of caring, Cat."

Although if they could, I can only imagine their views. Slowly, I shake my head. "Just in case – I don't want you to see that."

"Then I'll wait in the car." Her voice is gentle, but firm as she weaves our fingers together. "I won't let you go alone."

"He's not going alone."

Cat's eyes flicker, and she turns to Dante. Jaw tight, he nods to me from the doorway. "Ready when you are."

I glance between them, my eyes lingering on Caterina. "Come."

The word slips out impulsively, but I feel better for it. I want her with me for this. Dante stiffens, before he turns and disappears. "He—,"

"I know," she snaps. But she squeezes my hand. "He loves me. And I love him, but he's being an *ass*. Doesn't matter – I'm still coming."

Tossing the keys that Luc gave me, I follow her out into the bright sunshine and over to the sleek gray Maserati. Even Dante looks reluctantly impressed as he scans it. "The GranTurismo. Nice."

I bite my tongue before getting behind the wheel, and I wait.

And wait.

The argument, hushed and furious, rages on for long minutes, and I pull out my phone, sending a message to Luc's new phone.

The response has me grinning as the passenger door opens. Dante swears under his breath before yanking the seat down and climbing into the back.

The extremely *small* back.

The grin continues to tug at my lips as I turn to look, and he scowls at me. His legs are pulled up, twisted awkwardly. "Why are you so happy?"

I snap a photo, ignoring his irritated curse as I reply to Luc. "Because Luc bet on you to get the front seat, and I bet on Cat. To see who was the most stubborn. He owes me a hundred."

Cat slides gracefully into the car, pointedly not looking into the back. "At least you had faith in me."

"Luc thought you'd let him have it, so he didn't whine the whole way."

"*I do not whine.*"

Cat scoffs as I pull away from the house. I listen to their bickering as we drive, grateful for the distraction.

This visit... it will not be pleasant.

We arrive too soon, and I lean out of the window to scan my watch at the gate for entry. Ahead of us, the villa, a double storey white stone building covered in flowers, looks deserted at first glance.

"Are you sure they're home?" Cat leans forward, worrying her bottom lip.

"They're home." I park outside the main doors. No staff come out to greet us. Aside from a cleaner once a week, and a private chef that comes every few days at Rosa's insistence, my parents dismissed all of the staff when they first arrived.

I sit there for a moment, staring at the sandy-colored steps. They're worn away now, the sharp edges blunted by years of running up and down them. Chasing my sisters in and out of the house when we were younger, often sunburnt and hungry and laughing. Then, as we grew older, they started chasing me, wanting me to join in games that I no longer had any interest in. I was the Fusco heir. I had *responsibilities*.

I would play every single damn game with them now.

Forever feels inevitable, the world endless, when you're a child. And then it shrinks as you grow, until that infinity shrinks into days that are counted too quickly, hours of happiness that fly past without noticing.

By the time you start to care, by the time it *matters*, the moments have already passed.

You never know how much time you will have.

I glance in the mirror. Dante meets my eyes, understanding lingering in his green gaze.

Cat's hand slips into mine. "What do you need?"

Lifting her hand, I press my lips to her wrist. "You. Always."

She stays close, Dante at my back as we walk inside. The door is unlocked, the hall a familiar mix of eclectic furniture and paintings collected by my mother over the years. I frown at the thin layer of dust coating the sideboard.

"Ma?" I call out, glancing up at the stairs. "Padre? Rosie?"

Footsteps sound above our heads. "Gio?"

We all look up. Rosa hangs over the railing, her mouth falling open. "You're here?"

I offer her a small smile. "Surprise, Rosie."

We did not leave on the best of terms back at home. Staying where I am, I wait to see how she'll react. Her eyes travel over Cat, widening, and then to Dante. Behind us.

I wonder if I notice her shoulders sag. But she's flying down the stairs, and I stagger back as she hits my middle. Inhaling, I wrap my arms around my youngest sister. "I missed you."

She aims a punch at my arm, her face pulling into a familiar pout. "You *sent* me here. I want to come home, Gio."

"You know you can't." I step away, my eyes running over her face. "How are they?"

Her shoulders sag, eyes darting to Cat. "The same. Maybe... maybe a little worse. This house is full of ghosts, Gi. *Please*."

"Not yet." My tone is hard, and Rosie blinks. "This isn't a game. What's happening there... it is no safe place for you. Soon, but not now."

She studies my expression, but it's Cat that she swings to. "Is... is everyone well?"

My brows scrunch together as Cat takes her time putting her words together. "Yes. Vincent... says hello."

She makes no mention of the shot he took at the Asante estate. Studying my sister's flushed cheeks, I decide that is absolutely for the best.

I like Vincent. It would be a shame to kill him.

"Rosie," I nudge the discussion into more neutral territory. "Why don't you take Cat and Dante into the kitchen? Make a coffee. I'll join you shortly."

"Sure." She pauses. "They're not good, Gi. Just... prepare yourself."

Cat's hand silently brushes mine as she follows, glancing over her shoulder before they disappear out of sight.

Beside me, Dante sighs before he follows. "Call if you need us."

"*Grazie.*"

My feet feel heavy as I make my way upstairs. I pass my childhood bedroom, Rosa's room... and pause, my eyes landing on a door.

It looks the same. Battered romance novels fill the space from floor to ceiling, uneven stacks precariously placed against the wall and bursting out of the bookcase. Her dressing table is clean, her bed freshly made.

She hadn't been here for months before she died, but her scent still lingers, the patchouli oil she was obsessed with.

I stop beside the bed, bending to pick up the photograph.

None of us are looking at the camera, besides Nicci. Her face is squished into the corner, grinning. At our kitchen table, Rosa and I are arguing over the rules of a game, playing cards scattered around us as her finger jabs into my face. My parents watch on with slightly exasperated smiles, their hands linked.

A different life.

My heart feels heavy as I set it down, adjusting it minutely. There's no dust in this room, I realize suddenly. This room is kept spotless. Preserved.

As if waiting for someone that will never come home.

I knock on their bedroom door, waiting for a response that doesn't come before pushing the door open. "Mamma? It's me. Gio."

The room is dark and warm. My mother is alone, a dark bundle on the bed that faces the wall and doesn't turn. I sweep my gaze across her table, the plastic bottles scattered there. Some of them are full. Most are not. "Mamma."

I cross to the bed, dropping down to one knee. My mother blinks at me. Her hair hangs around her face, older than I remember it. "Gio."

I nod around the lump in my throat. And my mother... she starts to cry. Silent, wracking sobs that make her body shake as she reaches a trembling hand to her bedside table, searching blindly for the small bottle and opening it.

"You don't need those." But she pulls her hands away from mine, shaking out two white tablets and swallowing them dry.

"I need Nicci."

At the slurred words, a heavy weight settles in my chest. "I know."

"You took her from me."

A knife to the chest would hurt less than those words. "Joseph Corvo—,"

"*No,*" she snaps it, sagging back against her pillow. "You. You, Carlos, the *Cosa Nostra*. All of you, with your politics and your games and your wars. I told Carlos, but he wouldn't listen. The Cosa Nostra took my children from me and sent them back in pieces."

"Rosa is still here," I say hoarsely. "She needs you, mamma."

I try to take her hand, but it clenches into a tight fist.

"Get away," she hisses. "Get away from me."

Her voice rises to a shriek, and I back away as she presses her palms against her eyes, blocking me out. "Leave us alone. Leave us *alone*."

My heart shreds beneath the weight of her grief, her anger. My strong, vibrant mother huddles back into the bed, shaking and crying as I feel for the door and yank it open, closing it behind me.

My face burns, my body tingling as I sit on the floor and listen to my mother cry.

You took her from me.

The accusation weighs heavily, sinking down around my shoulders.

Soft footsteps. And when she settles next to me, her hand slipping into mine, I grip it tightly. "She thinks it's my fault."

"This does not sit with you." Cat stares at the wall opposite, her thumb running over the back of my hand. "The responsibility is ours, Gio. The Corvo line."

"Not yours," I say roughly. "We are not accountable for the sins of our families, Cat. It took me too long to work that out."

She sighs, resting her head back against the door. "We're going to get him."

"Yes." She sits with me, quiet, as I work through my own grief. Behind us, my mother eventually goes silent. Cat's head rests against my shoulder.

"Your father?" she asks eventually.

I stare down the hall. "He'll be in his office. Wait for me?"

"Always." She draws up her knees as I stand, brushing myself down.

My father was always a stickler for appearance. I doubt it will make a difference today.

Not bothering to knock, I walk straight in.

My father is slumped over his desk. Thick gray scruff covers his lower face and neck, his eyes bleary as he looks up. He doesn't say anything as I incline my head.

"Padre."

He picks up his glass, takes a deep swig of amber liquid. The smell of it hangs in the air around him, clings to his crumpled clothes, the stained shirt. "You're here."

A disinterested statement, as he stares at the bottle that now occupies most of his days. Stepping closer, I inspect the bottle too. Reach out to lift it.

A hand slams down over my wrist. "Leave it."

We lock gazes. I don't let go.

My father releases my hand only to yank open a drawer and pull out another bottle. He doesn't bother with the glass this time. "Why are you here?"

I study him. "You're going to drink yourself to death."

He takes another swig rather than answering.

"You have another daughter. You are *failing* her."

Silence. He doesn't meet my gaze, and anger prickles the back of my neck. "You have a family to take care of."

"They don't want me," he says finally. "Nor do you, *capo*."

I grit my teeth at the bitter twist there. "Do not judge me for stepping up to take on a role that you were incapable of filling. I see *nothing* that tells me I was wrong."

I'm wasting my time. My father is not ready to listen. Too lost in the alcohol, in the haze that consumes him daily.

"I'm cutting you off," I say quietly. "An allowance will be made for food and brought to the house. There will be no alcohol. I will arrange a nurse for mamma, to work on getting her off the meds."

His hands clench on the glass in his hand. "You can't do that."

"I can, and I will." My jaw hardens. "As you pointed out, I am the Fusco capo now. You will no longer have access to the accounts. And nor will Rosa. If I hear of you pressuring her, I will come back here and it will not end well."

"*Stronzo*," he hisses. "It should have been *you*, not her."

My back straightens. My father opens his mouth, closes it again before looking away.

"Rosa does not deserve to lose her parents too." My voice raises, hardens into ice. "I know you are grieving. We are *all* grieving. I refuse to allow you the luxury of losing yourself in the bottom of a bottle as the rest of your family suffers for it. Hate me for that by all means, if it makes you feel better. If it makes you feel *anything*."

"Get out," he says tightly.

Gladly. I can't stay here for a moment longer, watching him spiral into self-destruction as my mother overdoses down the hall and my sister walks on eggshells in a house filled with death.

"Nicci would be disappointed in you, Giovanni, to see you treat me like this."

My hand grips the doorknob.

I think of my sister. Of her quiet nature, and her big heart.

"Perhaps." I don't look back. "But you and I both know that she would be more disappointed in you."

I meet Cat's eyes as I step out. She's leaning against the wall, waiting.

A woman who would walk through fire for me. As I would for her.

And that ball of guilt and shame in my chest – it lifts a little, as I take her hand. Because I know that my little sister, with her dreams and her romantic heart, would not be disappointed in me for this choice, at least.

"She would have loved you," I say quietly. Sadly.

Her gaze is soft. "I think she would have been *very* protective of her big brother. But I hope so."

Rosa stands as we enter the kitchen. There's an apology on my face as our eyes meet. For sending her here, condemning her to days alone in this house.

"Soon." I mean it. "As soon as I can, Rosie, you're coming home. I swear it."

She deflates, but her arms wrap around me anyway, her face buried in my chest. "If it's not soon enough, I'll buy the ticket myself."

I run a hand over her back before pulling out my wallet. Sliding out a card, I hand it to her. "Here."

She turns it over in her fingers, a questioning look on her face.

"I'm cutting him off from the accounts," I tell her firmly. "Groceries will be delivered daily, but no alcohol, Rosie. Keep it hidden for anything you might need."

She nods, slipping it into her pocket. And then she winks, even if it looks a little wobbly. "I'm feeling a shopping spree in my near future."

"Have at it." I cup her cheek. "Soon. Okay?"

"Okay."

Luciano

"Are they back yet?"

At the gruff voice, I turn my head. We're sprawled on the rug in the living area, Alessia grabbing for every one of the million toys I ordered, inspecting them as I assess her reaction.

The *keep* pile is much, much bigger than the *toss* pile.

Dom lingers in the doorway, his eyes flicking down to watch her.

"Not yet. Come in."

He settles into a chair opposite us, hands gripping the sides as if he would rather be anywhere else.

I switch my attention back to Alessia as she holds up a teddy, shaking it with delight. "*Ba!*"

Stefano will be delighted to know that she sees him on the same level as a stuffed bear. When she climbs awkwardly to her feet, the teddy gripped in her small hand, I don't stop her as she wobbles across the room.

Dom goes still as she reaches him. He doesn't move, barely breathes, as she pushes the teddy into his lap with an expectant babble. She tries to climb up after it, letting out a frustrated noise when she slides back to the ground.

He stays still, gray eyes sliding to me as the noises from her mouth begin to border on upset. "Come and get her."

"Busy, I'm afraid." I press a white note on the little keyboard. "Lots of nursery rhymes to learn if I'm going to steal Stefano's spot as the favorite."

"*Luc.*"

I glance over my shoulder. "She wants you to pick her up."

"Morelli." He sounds almost tortured.

I press another key, ear cocked to hear the note. "Your sister must have been an amazing woman, Domenico."

Ice coats his tone. "What do you mean?"

I tilt my head toward Alessia, as she tries desperately to gain his attention. "Because there is a part of her that remains, in that little girl. She loves so *freely*, forgives mistakes without question or thought or fear, and that can only be because of how she has been raised. It is a wonderful gift to leave behind, I think. A small part of Beatrice, and her husband."

Dom's brow furrows as he looks down. He swallows, his throat bobbing.

I turn my attention back to the keyboard.

And the frustrated noises vanish, replaced by happier, flowing, nonsensical conversation.

When my phone goes off, I roll over to grab it, sitting up. "Nico."

"Luc." My second's voice is strained, more than I've ever heard it. "Something was sent through. A message. For you."

"For me—,"

I stop. Matteo would not have this number. Only the one I gave to Stefano, and that phone was lost in the Asante compound. "Send it through."

He hesitates. "It's not—,"

"*Send it through.*"

"What is it?" I don't respond to Dom's demand as the video loads. The hair lifts on the back of my neck as I press the screen.

No greeting awaits me. No words.

This is a different sort of message.

Dom is in front of me, his hand cupped over Alessia's head. "The fuck is *that*?"

In my hand, the screaming rings out. Endless screaming, over and over again. Thuds, cries. The video is dark, but I don't need to see to know exactly what this message is.

Domenico pales. "Is that—,"

"The price," I say numbly. The video ends, but I can still hear those fucking screams of agony, every single one burning into my soul and leaving scars behind.

Amie.

CATERINA

I know something is wrong as soon as we walk in.

The hall is silent. Luc sits at the bottom of the steps, his head in his hands.

Dante and I both burst into movement at the same time, Gio a step behind us.

"*What happened—,*"

"*Is she—,*"

"She's fine." We both spin, and the oxygen abandons my lungs at the sight of Dom, with Alessia in his arms. Stefano is beside him, his expression carefully controlled. I hold back as Dante goes to him, lifting her and running his hands over her as if checking for injuries.

"What's happened," I breathe. Not a question. Because *something* has put that look on Luc's face – that hollow, dead-eyed look as he lifts his head.

Slowly, he holds up a phone, his hand trembling as he presses the screen.

My muscles lock into place at the screaming that rings out.

Agony. There is nothing but sheer, unrelenting agony in those sounds, barely even human, and as I stare at Luc, I understand.

"Amie," I breathe raggedly. "That's Amie."

He nods. "A message was sent. To me."

Because he betrayed Matteo – made him think they were allies, friends even, and then he tricked him by stealing Alessia from under his nose with Amie's help.

And Amie has paid the price.

My hand presses against my ribcage. We waited too long. Waited, to *rest*, and all the while—

"We have to go," I whisper. "We have to go now."

"She's already dead." Luc's voice is harsh, and next to me, Gio flinches. "He doesn't fuck around, Cat. He doesn't need her. Amie is *dead*."

I shake my head. That's not right, can't be right, but as I look at Dom, he nods. His eyes are dark. "I'm sorry, Cat. But I agree with him."

I try to clear my head of the buzzing, to think around the pain in my heart. "Was there a video? Photos?"

Luc shakes his head. "The screaming wasn't enough?"

"Then she's not dead," I insist, my throat tight. "He wouldn't miss an opportunity to show us, Luc. She's still alive."

Even if she might wish it otherwise. My heart twists, convulses inside my chest. "*We have to go.*"

"We don't have a plan." Gio turns to me. "We need one."

My voice is short. "What if I have one already?"

They all turn in my direction.

"What?" Dante's voice is tight. "What plan?"

Sudden understanding hits me like a punch to the abdomen. "I...,"

I force myself to meet Luc's eyes. "I cut him off. Matteo. I have a hacker – a talented one. He broke in and transferred everything out of the Corvo accounts. Locked them down, so Matteo can't even get in. He no longer has access to any of the Corvo funds."

If he has no funds, he can't pay the men he's hired to kill us. There is no loyalty among the mercenaries of our filthy underworld.

Not all battles are fought with guns and knives.

Gio whistles. "Seems to be the day for it."

"When?" Luc swipes a hand down his face. "When did this happen?"

"This morning," I say quietly. I meet his shadowed eyes. "So you can save some of that guilt for me."

A retaliation. Payment in kind.

"He is cut off," I continue slowly. "He won't be able to sustain the numbers he currently has when he has no money to pay them. As they fall off, it gives us an opportunity, if we can get him out in the open. We push him toward that and hit him with everything we have."

"And Amie?" Luc says quietly.

"Perhaps we can make a deal." I consider options, flicking through them in my head. "He will be getting desperate. Desperation leads to sloppiness. But storming the Corvo estate is not a battle we will win, Luc. We did it once. He'll be expecting it, and will prepare for it. Better to meet him on ground he doesn't know as well."

"And where will that be?" Dante asks sharply. "Have you planned that yet?"

My eyes narrow. "I have some ideas."

"Excellent." He brushes past me, heading for the stairs. "Let me know when we're leaving, won't you?"

I resist the urge to snap back at him as he jumps the steps two at a time. Alessia's laughter trickles down to us before a door slams upstairs.

"My mother returns in two days." Luc gets to his feet as well. "That gives us two days to pull everything we need together. Work on the details."

"I need Cat for a few hours tomorrow afternoon." Dom's face doesn't change when I turn, but he crosses his arms. "It's not negotiable."

I scan his face. His gray eyes deepen as he meets my look with a steely one of his own. "Not negotiable."

My lip twitches upward. "Okay, then."

Everyone disperses, but I watch as Luc sits down on the step again. When I approach, he doesn't look at me. "I left her behind to face that, Cat."

"She made a decision," I say softly. "She knew what she was risking, Luc, and she made the choice anyway. There was nothing you could have done that wouldn't have ended up with all three of you paying the price."

Luc and Alessia would not have gotten out if it weren't for Amie. And I am grateful, more grateful than I can ever form words for, that she made that choice rather than risk their safety.

"Sometimes," I study the floor. "I wish we could just... go. Leave it all behind, Luc. The fighting, the politics – just fuck it all and go somewhere peaceful, where the Cosa Nostra is just a story."

His attention lingers on me. "Is that something you want?"

"It would be easier," I admit. "But the people we would leave behind – the fighting that would break out. I couldn't do that to them. But we can be better, Luc. The Cosa Nostra used to stand for something more than just a power grab."

Family. Loyalty. Honor.

"A better world," he murmurs. "How altruistic of you, little crow."

There will always be power. But what you do with it – how you use it – that matters. *More than I ever realized.*

"That's what I want," I say quietly. "A better world."

DANTE

I lay on my back, staring at the ceiling.

Soft, sniffling snores fill the air, and I look down at Alessia. She curls against my side, her face hidden by her wild curls and her thumb slack in her mouth.

I thought I knew what this would feel like. What *I* would feel like, when I finally laid eyes on her. But this feeling – it threatens to overwhelm me, even now.

The only thing missing is Cat.

I trace my finger over her hair. "Your mother is the most stubborn woman in the world, *tesoro mio*. Always making me hunt her down."

Careful not to wake her, I slide my hands beneath her sleeping form, lifting her into the cot Luc and I put together. I take a moment to fiddle with the screen next to it, slipping the monitor into my pocket.

The house is quiet as I move through. Dinner was subdued, all of us lost to our own thoughts. Even Luc was silent, his face grim as he ate before excusing himself.

This war is taking its toll. Continues to take it, even now, when we are back together. When Cat is back.

I search until I reach the small set of steps on the far side of the courtyard. They stagger down, leading directly into the sea.

And several feet out, Cat is floating, her hair a halo around her as she stares up at the sky.

She knows I'm here. I can tell by the stiffness of her expression as I toe off my shoes. My clothes.

I leave my underwear on, wading into the water.

We float beside each other. Above our heads, the sky is a sea of inky black. No stars are out tonight.

"I—,"

"I—,"

We both stop. She huffs, the smallest sound of amusement. "Go on."

"I was angry."

She waits.

"I'm sorry," I murmur. "My temper gets the better of me too often. And it feels as if I have been *angry* for so long that it's hard to switch it off, Cat. We have lost so much time, and I'm angry at that. I'm angry that Matteo is still out there. I'm angry... I'm angry that you had to save yourself, and we were too late to stop him from hurting you."

She's watching me now.

It spills out in waves of fury that burn my throat on the way out. "I'm angry that my father is dead, and he didn't deserve to go like that. I'm angry that this will not be over without more pain, more loss, when we have sacrificed *enough*. And I'm so angry that these days might be the only time we have, *tentazione*."

"And I'm *scared*, Cat. I'm scared of losing you. I'm scared that you'll run into danger and leave us behind, and we might not get you back this time."

I take a breath. "I want to fight with you every day for the rest of our lives. I want to argue with you, and fight over the front seat, and bicker over little things that don't really matter because the only thing that matters is us being together."

Her breath hitches.

"And I need your help." My voice is quieter now. "Because that little girl we made is a stubborn ball of fire, and she's going to need both of us to stay alive until the end of this, Cat. She's perfect, and she's ours, and it's hurting my heart to watch you holding yourself back when I can see how much it's hurting *you*."

I force my feet down to the floor, stand up in the water and turn to her, water dripping from my bare skin in the warm night air. Her face glows with the light from the courtyard behind us. "We get one life, Cat. I want to spend as much of it as I can with you, with her, even with this strange family that you've built."

I push my way toward her, cutting through the water, and grip her cheeks between my hands.

She's cold beneath my touch – *like ice*. "Cat."

And her eyes – they're glassy, as she stares straight through me. As if it's not me she's seeing at all. My body tenses as I look over my shoulder, and back to her.

She starts to shake.

"Hey." I drop my palms to her arms, rub up and down, trying to transfer some of my heat into her. "Talk to me."

She just stares. Stares at my bare skin, and I start to panic. "Look at me."

I try to pull her closer, and she... she *explodes*.

Her hands claw at my face, raking down my cheek as she throws herself back, disappearing under the water.

"Cat!" I roar her name, throwing myself after her. Her legs thrash as I drag her back up. "What the *hell*—,"

She's wheezing, pushing away from me, and my heart rips down the middle at the petrified look on her face. "*Stop – stop—,*"

I let go, backing away with my hands in the air. "*Tentazione*. Please. It's just me. Dante. *Your* Dante."

My heart is splintering at the fear that crosses her face. I thought I had seen her frightened, that night that she left us.

But not like this. *Never* like this.

CATERINA

I can't breathe.

Can't breathe – can't—

A black canopy.

A bare back.

The sky above my head. Flashes of bare skin. Heat on my arms, close, too close—

My world vanishes into cold, the buzzing in my ears dulling as my nose burns. And then those hands are on me again, pulling me up, shaking me. My name rings in my ears, called in panicked tones.

Fuck. Fuck—

I heave, doubling over as I wrap my arms around myself. I can't look at him. "Put – put your shirt on. *Please.*"

I stay like that, trying to catch my breath as he throws himself away from me. Seconds, countless seconds as I focus on breathing until he makes his way back to me.

"Cat," he breathes in anguished tones. His hands are up, stretching toward me, but he doesn't come closer. "Tell me what that was."

My panicked breathing turns to shudders. "No."

"Tell me," he says again, his voice hoarse with panic. "Tell me so I can make sure it *never* happens again."

I scared him. Scared myself.

My throat aches when I finally speak. "When I was – there. He kept injecting me with ket. Over and over again. And I couldn't remember what happened, not properly – I stopped knowing what was real and what wasn't."

His fists clench, but he waits, his eyes on mine.

"I would have these dreams," I say brokenly. "All the time. Where I would see you – all of you, and we would be living a normal life, and it was perfect. And then it would twist, and change, and I couldn't work out if I was awake or asleep."

His face crumples, agony crossing it. "*Tentazione*."

But I hold up a hand. If I stop, I don't think I'll be able to start again.

"But I kept seeing the same thing, over and over again. This black canopy above my head, and – and a bare back."

Slowly, he looks down. And then up, at the sky.

I grip myself, my nails digging into my arms. "That – that was real. It was *him*, sleeping, and I was just... laying there, and I knew what had happened. Maybe I thought he was one of you – or maybe I was too out of it to realize, but I don't remember fighting it. He took what he wanted, and I couldn't stop him. I didn't stop him."

Nausea surges, my hand slamming over my mouth until it passes. I swallow several times and take a breath.

"I don't remember the details. And maybe that's a good thing. Maybe it isn't. And I still – I still *want* you. All of you. I was with Luc before, and he kept his shirt on and it was fine. I'm *fine*. Just – that's a bad combination for me."

I grip my elbows, falling silent.

The water sloshes as he moves closer. "Can I...?"

I nod. Stare at the soaked cotton of his white shirt as he moves to stand in front of me. He takes my fingers and presses it to his chest. "Do you feel this?"

His heartbeat pounds beneath my touch, and I nod again.

Carefully, he leans forward, until our foreheads press together. And when he speaks, there's an edge to his voice that I haven't heard before. "This is the heartbeat of a man who loves you with everything he is, Caterina Corvo. I want to *kill* him for what he did to you. Rip him apart with my bare fucking hands, but you did that already. Don't you dare stand there and tell me you didn't fight, when he is dead and you're standing here in front of me."

My lungs feel a little less tight at his words.

"He took something from me," I admit. "I'm not the same person that I was three months ago."

"None of us are the same people we were." His heartbeat thumps against my palm, as if confirming the truth of his words. "But your heart hasn't changed, Cat."

"A little more fragile, maybe."

"Then I will look after it more carefully." His lips press to my forehead. "What do you want, Cat?"

I think about it. And he gives me that space, waiting patiently as if we have all the time in the world, both of us standing in water at the edge of the sea.

And in the end, the answer is surprisingly simple. "I want to be happy."

"Then focus on that." He half-smiles, sadness and anger still lingering in his eyes. "Do more of what makes you happy. Not everything has to be a battle."

We walk slowly back to the house. Dante slides the monitor out of his pocket, checking it. "She's asleep?"

He nods. And my hand tightens around his. "Will you stay with me tonight?"

Dante swallows. "You've never asked me that before, you know. Not out loud."

Maybe I need to be a little more careful with his heart, too.

So I lead him to my bedroom. My damp feet sink into the rug as I pull off my swimming costume. He hesitates. "Give me a minute."

He's gone for the few minutes it takes to brush my teeth, slipping inside. My eyes skate over the fresh, dry shirt, my heart squeezing.

"Tell me," he rasps. "If you feel – if there's *anything*."

I want his skin against mine. Want to feel him all around me. He balks when I unbutton the front of the shirt, but I only press my lips to his bare chest. "Just the back."

Dante follows me down onto the bed, our bodies slotting together in perfect connection. He tangles his fingers with mine, his lips moving over my mouth, my neck. My breasts, his tongue rasping over my nipples, sealing over them and sucking until my back bows.

He pauses to kiss the brand in my skin before he continues down. And my stomach flexes as he examines the marks there, in the low golden light of the lamp next to the bed. His lips are reverent as they travel over me, as if he's learning me all over again. His fingers dip, feeling the wetness between my legs as he strokes, the pad of his finger rubbing against my clit.

And when I've had enough, when I can't wait anymore, I pull him up, his mouth on mine as he pushes inside me with excruciating gentleness.

We don't speak, our breathing the only sound as he moves inside me, our eyes locked together. As if neither of us wants to break this moment.

My fingers brush his cheek. Push back his growing hair. "*Ti amo.*"

"*Ti amo.*" He wraps his arms around me as he comes, my body twisting beneath his as his face buries in my neck. "Forever, *tentazione.*"

Domenico

My knuckles smash into the bag hanging from the ceiling, over and over again.

"Looking to break some bones?"

I don't stop at the quiet question. Instead, I hit harder. "If I wanted your opinion, I would have fucking asked for it."

I don't tell him that my sloppy position is intentional. That I'd welcome the pain of broken bones, take it with a smile and a fucking thank you over this damn buzzing in my head that screams at me to *fight*. To punch and smash until red flows beneath my hands.

Punching the hell out of this bag at least takes the edge off.

I drag the bag to a stop, pausing long enough to snag the water next to me and take a drink. Feeling eyes on me, I turn. "Problem?"

I came down to the gym for some peace and fucking quiet. It's not even six in the morning yet.

Stefano *fucking* Asante doesn't blink an eye at my tone. "I know what it feels like, you know."

I scoff at him, pulling the wraps from my hands and flexing them. "I don't want to be psychoanalyzed."

Cat may have chosen the fucker, but it doesn't make us friends.

But he doesn't move. "I know what it is like to be made into something you never wanted to be, Rossi. You want to fight it out, I'll get on the mat with you."

I narrow my eyes, assessing him. "You might not walk back off."

I'm not exaggerating. And the fucker makes a show of looking me up and down, before he raises his eyebrow. "I'm not worried."

I point to the open space in the center of the gym. "Rules?"

He shrugs. "Not particularly a fan of them. I won't kill you, though. Cat wouldn't be happy."

Something that might be amusement sounds at the back of my throat. "Feel free to try. I don't plan on holding back."

He peels off his shirt, rolling his shoulders before he joins me. I eye the artwork inked over his neck. Must have been someone with skill.

I stretch out my swollen knuckles.

He notices my stare. "Want to touch? Buy me dinner first."

"Fuck you. No wonder you never used to speak."

Stefano bounces back on his feet, his eyes noting my position, the hold of my arms. He seems to know what he's doing, at least.

Something he proves when I move, sudden and swift. My right arm swings up in a savage blow that would be a clean KO, but he easily sidewipes it with surprising agility.

Warier now, we circle each other.

"Come on," he flicks his fingers at me. "Go for it. You know you want to, Rossi. Better to get it out here."

I wait for him to move back, for his foot to lift so he's off balance, before I strike again. Back and forth we go, neither of us able to land a true hit on the other.

Frustrated, I lunge for his left side, and he shoves me back.

"Tell me, Asante. Did she scream when you *branded* her?"

He stumbles, and my next blow lands directly in his ribs. "Better me than any of the others. I've seen too many die from that fucking rod to let anyone else place it on her."

"Fuck you," I hiss at him, lowering my hands. "So I should be – what? Grateful? You've *scarred* her. She'll have to look at that brand every day for the rest of her goddamned life, Asante. What else did you do to her that isn't so obvious?"

His sudden blow smashes into my cheek, and I stumble back. He advances on me, hands up defensively.

"I did everything I could," he says abruptly. "He had my mother, Rossi – you've seen her. My hands were fucking tied, and I *still* risked her life to get Cat out of there."

"He drugged her." I shove him back, smash him in the face. "Fuck knows what else. Don't tell me you did everything you fucking could. What did you do, kiss her forehead in apology as he was injecting her?"

"I was *locked up*!" He roars the words at me, his voice bouncing around the room. "He locked me in a fucking cell for forty-six days to keep me away from her. You think I don't feel that guilt, that she had the chance to leave and *she came back*? You think I didn't try to rip those bars apart to get to her?"

We both stop. He doesn't look away. A cut has opened up above his eyebrow, splitting the skin as blood drips and he wipes it away impatiently.

"I spent forty-six days *listening*," he says heavily. "Listening to the soldiers talk about her. About what he was doing to her. And sometimes, he'd come and tell me himself. It was fun for him to do that, to torture me, knowing I couldn't do anything but sit on my fucking ass as he walked back up there to do it again. I remember every single fucking second of that time, and it kills me. She cannot remember it, but I can't fucking escape it. You don't need to punish me, Rossi. I already have a fucking life sentence, because I will *never forget*."

Red mist drops over my vision at the look on his face.

"What did he do?" Hoarse words, ripped from my chest.

He shakes his head, face resolute. "That's not my place. If I tell anyone, it'll be Cat. If and when she asks, but she doesn't need those fucking details in her head. So I will try my fucking best to forget them, and to be the man she makes me *want* to be, instead of Salvatore's fucking creature. You should do the same."

He stalks off the mat before he turns back to me. "I don't owe you my guilt, Rossi. You've got enough of your own."

He walks away and leaves me there. I grip the back of my head, trying to push that red mist away but it just gets darker.

I came down here to try and work this fucking buzz off, to ease that craving for violence before I see her later. But all it's done is raise something savage inside my head.

I make for the small bathroom that adjoins the underground gym, and switch on the light.

The bruising looks worse in this light. I may as well be a patchwork fucking quilt.

I stare at the mirror.

One moment, it's there. Whole.

And the next, it shatters around me, glass showering the steel basin until I can see twenty warped versions of my own reflection in the shards left behind.

I punch it again. Again. And I'm shouting, roaring over that agony in my head, in my fucking heart, as I look down at that glass.

I failed her. I failed her so badly, and I'm still fucking failing her.

Hands grab at my arm, and I turn, swinging my fist.

It smashes into a solid grip, even as horror locks my muscles into stillness, the fury draining and fear taking its place within a second. "*Merda*, Cat—."

Her hand stays wrapped around my fist as we stare at each other. It must have hurt – her fucking wrist, the strain of catching that punch—

She looks down at the broken pieces, still holding onto me. "I did the same thing. Smashed my fists into my bathroom mirror at the Asante compound."

Her eyes are dark. "I picked up the longest, sharpest piece, and I considered how quickly I would bleed out if I dragged it along my wrist. Or if I was quick enough, would I be able to cut my own carotid?"

My breathing deepens, agony with every spike.

"I had to decide if it was worth fighting. Death is easy. Living – that's harder."

She's breaking my fucking heart. A heart I thought was broken already, as if she's sliding those shards into it.

"And then," she whispers, "I thought about what I would be leaving behind. What would happen, when you found out? Dante, Luc, Gio – what would they do? And I knew that wasn't something I *ever* wanted to think about again. What your faces would look like."

She shoves, and my back slams against the wall. The edge of a dagger pricks against my neck. "Don't you ever put that look on my fucking face, Domenico Rossi. Do you hear me? That's a fucking order."

"What did you do?" I rasp the words with effort. My hand twists in hers until I'm holding her. "With the mirror?"

She stands there, her chin lifted. "I chose to save my anger for those who deserved it. And that wasn't me. So I hid the sharpest pieces, and I waited until I could use those edges on *them*."

She smiles, and it's savage. Victorious. "I dragged that blade across Cecile's throat like butter. It took her so long to bleed out. And Salvatore – I used a steak knife, jagged and blunt, to carve a crow into his chest. To brand him, the way that he branded *me*. I sliced up every part of him that I could see. And then I cut off his cock."

Her lips tighten. "I made sure he felt every moment of what he had done to me. To us, Dom. So believe me when I tell you to save that anger. Save it for the person who fucking deserves it. And that person is not you."

I look down. "I—,"

"When a weapon is used," she says softly. "Who is to blame? The object that had no choice? Or the person who wielded it?"

She pulls herself back, her final words lingering in my head. Her face tightens as she looks down, and I follow her eyes to my bare chest. "The bruising is fading."

She smiles, but it's sad. "All things fade in time. We just need to weather it."

Swallowing, I rub my hands down my face. "I'll try. These thoughts – they're not easily dissuaded, Cat."

"No," she says quietly. "They're not."

CATERINA

Dom's voice stops me as I'm leaving. "Are you still... free later?"

I turn back to him. He's leaning against the wall, his eyes still filled with shadows and his knuckles trailing blood onto the concrete floor. "Are you asking me on a date, Domenico Rossi?"

His brows draw down. "Yes."

A date.

Do more of what makes you happy.

And suddenly, a date sounds... perfect. "I think I'm available. What do I wear?"

"Whatever you want." His voice rumbles as he pushes away from the wall. "You always look beautiful to me."

My stomach is still flipping as I walk up the stairs and into the bedroom. Dante is still asleep, one arm flung over his face, and my head jerks as a small noise comes from the corner.

Slowly, I cross the room. And I lean forward to pick up the monitor from the sideboard.

Alessia is awake. Wide awake, yanking on the bars of her crib. Something that sounds suspiciously like an off-key song echoes out, and my lips twitch into a smile.

I hold that monitor in my hands for a minute.

We never know how much time we will have.

The door closes softly behind me, the monitor dark in my hand as I slip into Dante's room. Alessia stops singing, her eyes following me as I crouch in front of her.

"That was a pretty song."

She eyes me with a freakishly familiar look. One of mine, if I'm not mistaken. And my smile slowly fills up my face as I gently tap the hand clinging to the top of the bars. "Shall we go for some breakfast, Alessia Corvo?"

I swear she purses her lips. I glance into the crib, spying a teddy, and hold it up. The paw brushes against her nose, and it wriggles.

When I do it again, her cheeks crease in a smile. "*Ba.*"

Carefully, awkwardly – I reach in and pick her up. She's heavy in my arms, a warm, sleepy bundle in her little sleep vest. And a heavy feeling diaper.

Nothing like learning on the job.

Two discarded diapers later, we're in the kitchen. I fumble with the clean beaker I found on the side, filling it with water, and place her into the highchair that appeared with Luc's ridiculously large order.

I sneak glances at her as I pull food from the fridge. Alessia plays with the teddy, yanking on its ears and shaking it around. "Ba."

"Ba," I test.

She frowns at me, unimpressed with my attempt. "*Ba.*"

I bite my lip to stifle the laugh that bubbles up. "You really are your father's daughter."

Bright green eyes blink at me.

The strawberries are partly a success. Some gets into her mouth, the rest on the floor. In her hair, mashed into her curls.

Everywhere.

I cut up another, slicing off a piece and offering it to her before popping the rest into my mouth. "Mmmm."

"Mmmmm-ah."

I blink. Try to ignore the sudden twist in my chest. She's only copying me.

But I say it again, unable to resist. "Mmmma."

"Mmmmma." She grins at me, delighted with this new game. "Ma!"

My throat feels suspiciously thick as I try to wipe up the red mush left behind, before lifting her back out of the chair. Sticky red hands immediately land on my cheeks, patting them. Alessia brings her nose close to mine. "*Ma.*"

"Ma," I whisper. "Clever girl."

I carry her across the hall, pulling open the door. The courtyard is still cool, shaded in the morning air as I carry her across to the steps. "Have you seen the sea yet?"

She ignores it completely as I sit on the top step, the warm water lapping against my toes, and settle her between my legs, her own small feet slipping into the water.

"Look." She stills as I lean forward, my palm gently slapping the water so it ripples. Gently, I cup some in my hand, using it to wash off her hands as she wriggles.

An excited squeal tears from her throat as she hits the top of the water, splashing herself *and* me. A laugh, bright and bubbly.

When I lean forward to create my own splash, she laughs harder, her whole body shaking with amusement.

And I realize very quickly that there is not much I wouldn't do to hear that laugh as much as possible. As *often* as possible.

Both of us are sitting fully in the water, Alessia a step above me as I hold her steady, by the time I hear movement behind me.

Dante's eyes glitter as he settles on the top step, his own feet bare.

"How long have you been watching?" I keep my eyes on Alessia.

"Long enough." His voice is thick as he extends the beaker from the kitchen to Alessia, and she grabs it, sucking on the water. He balances a fresh coffee on the top step. "I'll leave you be."

He starts to get up.

"Stay." I look up at him, watch as he slowly settles back down.

And then I flick water over him, Alessia cackling as he shakes his head in mock despair. He flicks the smallest bit of water over her legs, smiling as she laughs. "You won't have her as a shield forever, *tentazione*."

Grinning, I flick him again. "Oh, I'm counting on it."

CATERINA

I lean back in my seat. "It's not the strongest plan."

A lot of it hinges on my shoulders. "If I can't persuade the rest of the senior soldiers to follow me, we're going to struggle with numbers."

"Assuming Matteo's numbers drop as we hope they will, that might not be an issue." Gio leans forward, studying the rough sketch with a frown. "You think you can get him onto campus?"

"I don't think he'll be able to resist. Not if he already thinks he's won." My hair brushes against his as I lean in too, pointing at the hall we use for ceremonies. "We pin him down there."

Stefano clears his throat. "If there's anything left standing at the estate, there should be plenty of weapons. Ammunition. Gear."

"What of the rest of it?" Luc voices the question. "You're the Asante capo now. Like it or not, you'll need to decide."

Stefan's eyes flash to mine. "It's not a legacy I want. And the type of men Salvatore kept under him – you don't want them. Trust me."

"A clean out then," Dante says quietly. "You could start again, if you were of a mind to."

A bloody, drawn-out process. Stefano sighs. "Not a priority right now."

"Leave it too long, and a power vacuum will appear. They'll start scrabbling for scraps, and it will bubble over into smaller gang wars." I hold his gaze. "Most of his senior men died at the compound. The others will fall in line."

His jaw tightens. "I don't have a single ally in the Asante ranks. Not one."

"But you have five out here." Gio taps his fingers. "Admittedly, we can't stretch ourselves too thin right now. But when this is done, we can help you."

Dom shifts in his seat, but he doesn't say anything to dispute Gio's words.

Stefan's face twists. "Why would you do that?"

None of them speak. Luc eventually shrugs. "Family."

"Ba!" Alessia kicks her legs, and Stefan glances down at her. Swallows. "I… would appreciate that."

Family.

***

I take my time getting ready. Study the clothes Luc ordered, take the time to wash my hair and let it dry into waves that fall down my back.

I study myself in the mirror for far longer than necessary.

Don't be ridiculous, Caterina.

When the door knocks, it's a relief to pull it open. Dom lingers on the other side, smartly dressed in a deep blue shirt and cream chinos. He swallows, his eyes sweeping my body. "Perfect."

I smooth down the dress with an irritating amount of self-consciousness. The sweetheart A-line neck dips low, leaving my brand, my ruined crow tattoo on display. The green material hugs my waist, flaring out into a skirt that dips low at the back. "I actually forgot about the brand until I put it on. But I don't want to cover it up."

It would be another victory, another small hold over me, and I refuse to let them have it.

Dom's hand lingers in the small of my back as we walk. "I can design something to cover it. If you want to."

My hand reaches up to trace the puckered skin. "Maybe."

Dom leads me to the gray Maserati we drove to the Fusco estate, opening the passenger door and waiting. I grin at him as he climbs behind the wheel, and he narrows his eyes at me. "What is it?"

I turn to look out of the window. "Just... it's funny to see you being chivalrous, Domenico Rossi."

But... nice.

I turn back to him, sucking in a breath when I find his face close.

Warm lips close over mine. Dom's hand slides behind my neck, cupping it as he tastes me.

"Trust me," he says gruffly when he pulls away, "there is nothing *chivalrous* about the things I dream of doing to you, Cat."

Well. I press my lips together.

He keeps his hand on my knee as he drives, his thumb tracing tiny circles against my bare skin where my skirt rises up. By the time he pulls up, I'm trying not to squirm. He gives me a wry glance as he turns off the engine. "Feeling okay?"

I press my tongue into my cheek. "I'm enjoying the chivalry. But I'd *really* enjoy it if we slid the seats back and I climbed onto your lap."

The temperature rises as we stare at each other.

"Let me do this," he says finally, cupping my cheek. "I want you. It's been too long. But let me do this first. I want to take you on a date, Caterina Corvo. I want to push the rest of it out, just for a little while."

And I want to let him.

Our fingers tangle together as we walk down toward the beach. Ahead of us, the sun is setting, casting the sky in vivid shades of orange, pink and purple that takes my breath away. "It's beautiful here."

"Is it?" Dom's lips turn up. "I hadn't noticed."

"Why – *oh*." Heat rises on my cheeks. "You charmer, Rossi."

Dom's low laugh settles something in my chest. "I'm trying."

He's trying hard. My breath catches as he leads me around a corner, and I take it in. The large rug is scattered with colorful pillows, tall candles embedded in the sand around it. A cooler sits alongside.

"The sky isn't technically blue." Dom's voice is apologetic. "But there is sand, and the sea. And the sunset."

Memory flickers.

I don't remember him saying those words. But Stefan did, and repeated them back to me. Gave me hope that I didn't even realize how much I needed.

"Dom." My voice is thick. I don't – can't – say anything else. So I pull his face down to mine, kiss him deeply, trying to push everything I'm feeling – *too much* – into it.

My cheeks are wet when we break apart. He leads me to the blanket, opening the cooler to reveal an ice bucket and a chilled bottle of white wine. "You thought of everything."

He hums as he pours me a glass, pulling out a bottle of beer for himself. We settle against the pillows, my head on his stomach as we watch the colors move across the sky and deepen into rich, vivid red.

Dom plays with my hair as we talk – about memories, our childhood, about anything that isn't the bloody reality we're trying to forget, just for tonight.

I sit up as he lights the candles around us, the flickering amber lights sending shadows bouncing across his face as he leans down and fiddles with something next to the cooler.

My cheeks crease when the music starts. "I like this song."

"I know." He holds out his hand. "Dance with me, Caterina Corvo."

I'm going to dance with you as the sun sets.

The area around us is deserted, either by design or by chance. So there's nobody to see us as I rest my head against Dom's chest and we sway to the quiet melody, his arms wrapped around me as we face the setting sun, watching until the last rays disappear on the horizon.

"Full marks for you, Domenico Rossi," I whisper. "You've set the bar extremely high, you know."

He kisses the top of my head.

I tip my face up to his, catching his lips with mine before I glance around.

His brows dip as I take a step back, my hands rising to the back of my dress. "Caterina."

I tug at the zip, pulling it as far as I can before I turn, sweeping my hair back. "I need a little help."

His fingers brush against my skin. "Someone might see."

"Live a little." I suck in a breath as he drags the zip down, his lips following. My whole body heats as I feel the touch of his tongue. He tugs the zip down to just below my hips before pausing.

"You don't seem to be wearing any underwear."

His tone is wry, but there's heat flickering beneath as I turn, pushing the dress down until it slips to the floor. "I forgot it."

His arms band around me in the next second, lifting me before he lays me back against the blanket. My hand moves to the button on his chinos, but he bats my touch away. "My turn first. Hands up."

I stretch my hands above my head, curving my spine like a cat for his mouth as it travels over my skin. Letting him think he's won.

The noise he lets out as I wrap my legs around him and flip us is... satisfying. I grin down at him. "Stay."

"*Cat.*"

As I unbutton his shirt, his fingers grip mine. "I was going to keep it on."

I pause, my eyes moving to his. "Dante told you?"

"Not everything." His eyes sweep my face. "Just to leave it on. Was he wrong?"

Slowly, I shake my head. "Unbuttoned is fine."

I move down, my finger brushing the hard length beneath Dom's trousers as I undo his buttons, sliding my hand in and cupping him. "Looks like I'm not the only one who forgot my underwear."

He groans as I squeeze. His hips lift, letting me drag his trousers down. "When I thought about this, I was the one – *uh* – *playing* with you."

"Trust me." I trace my tongue down the underside of his cock. "You're not going to have any regrets, Domenico."

He bucks beneath me as my mouth seals over his head. "Definitely not."

I sink down until his head presses against the back of my throat before pulling back and finding a rhythm. Dom moves with me, hips twisting as I suck. He buries his fingers in my scalp, massaging. "No regrets. Not a single one."

I keep going as his hips move with greater insistence. I want to feel him release in my mouth, to lose control as I swallow him down. But he moves, sitting up as his hands slide to my waist, lifting. "Up."

My legs curl around his waist as I sink down onto him. His cock stretches my soaking pussy, my forehead pressed against his shoulder.

And then we're twisting again, Dom giving me a smug look as he flips us and pushes inside me, spreading my legs wide as my head tips back on a gasp.

With my thighs pushed apart, I feel every inch of him as he bucks into me, his chest pressed against mine. Our breathing turns to shuddering gasps in the cooling air. "Dom – I'm going to—,"

"Yes," he hisses. "Come around my cock, Cat."

My cry rings out, muffled by Dom's lips on mine as he presses into me with a groan. Wet heat spills as he comes with my name on his lips, filling me even as he keeps gently pumping his hips, pushing my tremors on for endless seconds.

He rolls onto his back, taking me with him as his hands run up and down my spine. We both try to catch our breath. "This was *not* an approved date activity."

"Don't make me take a point off." I bury my face in his skin, breathe him in as his hands skate down my back, over the cheeks of my ass and back up. "We needed this."

"We did." He finds my lips as we lay there, content with each other.

"I should get dressed," I whisper eventually. His hands eventually release me as he watches with heavy-lidded eyes, his arm propped behind his head.

I realize my error as I pull my dress back on. "I need to clean up."

Dom smirks at me. "No."

I stop, my hands on my zip. He hauls himself up and brushes my fingers out of the way, tugging it up before his lips press against the back of my neck. "You wanted to be fucked, Caterina. You can walk around full of me for the rest of the night."

I stare at him. "Seriously?"

He raises an eyebrow. "Do I not look like I mean it?"

I consider it. "Do we... have anywhere else to go?"

He shrugs, a smile playing around his mouth. "Maybe."

He ducks out of reach as I throw a punch at him. "So violent."

We pack up as the sun sets fully, taking it back to the car before he pulls me away. "We're not done just yet. A little walk, and then we'll head back."

I know I'm not imagining the amusement in his voice.

I swallow. "Just so you know, *you* are sliding down my leg."

At my words, he throws his head back, a genuine, loud laugh bursting from his mouth. I stop to stare at him. "I missed that."

His grin softens into something more tender. "I thought about what you said."

"Which part?"

"All things fade in time," he says quietly. "Good memories will outweigh the bad ones eventually."

"I'm not sure it works like that." Even though I wish it did.

"I know. But it doesn't hurt to build as many as possible."

We stroll down toward the marina, several people passing us on the way. They glance at me, at Dom, and promptly put distance between us and them.

I glance up at him. In the darkness, he looks nothing less than intimidating, the bulk of his shoulders, the muscles beneath his shirt obvious. And then there's the bruising. His lips quirk up. "Do I have something on my face?"

I look over my shoulder at the couple hurrying away from us. "Most know we still maintain a presence here. They're wary."

The Cosa Nostra may not have the power it used to in Sicily, but people have long memories.

He leads me into the marina and I take in the rows of yachts bobbing in the water. Most are dark, but he leads me down alongside them until we pause outside one of the biggest. "Remind me what they say about compensating?"

He grins, holding out his hand to help me up the gangway. Lights flicker up on the deck, and my ears prick at the low hum of conversation. "Who else is here?"

He doesn't say anything as we climb on board. The side deck is lit with floodlights as we make our way to the main observation deck on the upper level.

I stop short, my smile stretching.

Luc lounges back in his seat, a glass of wine hanging from his hand. "Did I hear you complaining about the size of my yacht, little crow?"

They're all here. Seated around the glass dining table, looking remarkably relaxed beneath the strings of lights above them. Gio holds up a beer in greeting. "Good surprise, I hope."

"It is." Dom pulls out a chair, and I settle between Gio and Stefan before looking at Dante. Dom slides into the seat beside him. "Where is she?"

He points, and I turn, spotting the playpen, the small bundle inside it. "She's asleep."

"She ate most of the food first, though." Luc pops an olive into his mouth. "But we saved some for you."

"Good." I reach out and snag the antipasti platter, dragging it toward me. "I seem to have worked up an appetite."

The smile playing around Dom's lips deepens. "I thought you were *full*."

I pick up a piece of *tara donne*, biting off the edge of the flatbread. "I seem to have space for more."

Luc points his glass at me. "Tell me why that sounded like something else."

"Ask Dom." I settle back in my seat, listening to Luc throw questions at Dom about our date which he refuses to answer. Low music plays around us, the low swish of the waves soothing as I sip at my wine.

Gio waits until I push the platter away before he pulls out the pack of cards. Dante groans. "Not again."

Gio raises an eyebrow at me. "I'll be better prepared this time." Then he looks over at Stefano. "She's a shark. Just to warn you, since nobody bothered to warn *me*."

"So is Luc," Dante mutters. "I happen to own ninety per cent of Las fucking Vegas. And she *still* wiped the floor with us."

Stefano turns dark eyes on me, considering. "Is that so?"

I shrug nonchalantly. "I'm not bad. And I'm not wearing any underwear, so—,"

I stiffen, my eyes flying to Dom. "Actually, excuse me for a moment."

But he stands. "Why don't you stay where you are?"

The flush curls over my skin. "*Dom.*"

But I stay in place as he heads inside, the others watching with curiosity. My cheeks are burning by the time he comes back outside. He leans in and murmurs in my ear. "Cheek against the table, Caterina. Since I made the mess, it feels only fair that I clean it up."

My stomach swoops, clenches.

Slowly, I lower myself to the table. Their attention focuses on me, their eyes sending flickers of heat across my skin. "That sounds... acceptable."

"Lower." I flush at the sound of Gio's voice. "Cheek against the glass, Caterina."

My palms, my face, I press them down against the cool glass in an attempt to ease my flaming face.

A warm palm slides up the back of my leg. Higher. And the cool air kisses my bare skin as he slowly pushes my dress up, flipping it over my hips.

"Look at you," he says, his tone full of primal satisfaction. "Stuffed full of me. You look perfect stuffed with my cum, *boss*."

I grit my teeth, even as my knees weaken.

Sneaky, sneaky bastard.

From my position, I can only see Gio. My eyes widen as he pushes his chair back. He offers me a smirk. "Only fair to share with the group."

"Jesus," I mutter. My heart stops as chairs screech and footsteps move around me. "Form an orderly line."

Laughter. Low, soft laughter as they gather around me. I crane my head to look.

Gio and Luc are standing there, shamelessly... *looking*.

I twist, catching Dante's eye. He pushes the sliding door open with a still-sleeping Alessia in his arms, disappearing inside, and I breathe a sigh of relief as he reappears with the monitor in his hand.

This is definitely *not* the lasting impression I want to leave my daughter with.

Dom strolls past me, settling back into his seat. He meets my look with a smirk. "I've had my fun. Thought I'd give you an extra point by watching instead."

But there's still someone missing. I turn my head, the glass warm now, and look for Stefan. He hasn't moved from his chair on my other side, his jaw tight.

"Stefano." There's a challenge in Gio's voice. But there's an invite, too.

I bite down on my lip as our eyes meet. The uncertainty in his gaze doesn't help the sudden panic that grips my stomach at the thought that maybe... maybe *this* isn't what he wants.

Five of them. Only one of me.

What if I'm not enough?

He reads my expression, and his eyes soften. "You *need* an army, Caterina. Nobody else would be able to keep up."

Luc's voice is dry. "I said something very similar, once."

But Stefan doesn't look away from me. "Is this... what you want? From me?"

I don't speak. I only nod, not trusting myself.

His hand brushes against my cheek as he stands, and that clenching in my stomach turns to something deeper as he joins them.

Fingers trace my slit, barely brushing it before a warm towel wipes over me. Dante speaks. "We don't have a bed big enough for all of us, so we're going to have to make do."

"A mistake I intend to rectify as soon as possible," Luc murmurs. "But in the meantime... how many of us can fuck you before your legs give out, little crow?"

My hands twist, searching for something to hold onto. "I'm pretty sure I can outlast all of you, Morelli."

A lie. An absolute, bald-faced fucking *lie*. It feels as though I'll combust as soon as they properly touch me.

"Big words. That sounds like a challenge." Gio. "What do you want if you win?"

I consider it. The fingers push against my entrance, testing, and I press my hips back in silent demand. "I quite like this yacht."

Luc whistles. "So do I. Challenge accepted."

"What do you get?" I jolt as those fingers slide into me, twisting and flicking as I push up onto my tiptoes. "If you win? Unlikely, of course."

The hoarse rasp of my words doesn't give off a huge amount of confidence.

The fingers disappear, and I hold my breath as I feel something thicker. Gio leans in, his words murmured directly into my ear. "If you could see what we see, you'd know that we've *already* won."

He slams into me, fingers gripping my hips, and my cry echoes into the air. I try to hold on as he sets a punishing rhythm. My toes scrunch, my panting making the table beneath me mist up. "Oh, *God*."

"Not God." Another slam, so deep I swear I can see fucking stars. "Say my name, *principessa*."

"Gio." I almost slur it as he increases his movements, my legs pushing further apart until he's almost holding me up, his fingers buried in my skin. "Fuck – yes. *Harder*."

"Merda," he hisses. "You're gripping my cock so fucking tightly, I'm not going to last."

"That's—," my words cut off with a moan as he moves one hand to my clit, pinching the already swollen bud. "—the *plan*."

I clench around him, squeeze him as hard as I can, and he roars into my neck, his chest pressing into my back as he finds his release. He spins me as I'm still catching my breath, his hands gripping either side of my face as he finds my lips.

"Alright, enough. I'm feeling a little competitive this evening." Luc's eyes sparkle as he nudges Gio aside. His thick cock is already in his hand, and he rubs over the barbells. His eyes trace my body, the small straps around my upper arms. "Let me see those pretty tits of yours, little crow."

I raise shaking fingers to the straps, yanking them down and reaching to tug at my zip until I can pull the top of my dress down and shimmy as it falls to the floor. My breasts spill free, and Luc groans, deep in his throat as he steps forward. I move to turn, but he stops me. "No. I want to see your face when I'm fucking you. Hands around my neck."

I raise my shaking hands, and he swoops in to brush his lips across mine. "All you need to do is hold on."

He slides his hands beneath my ass, hoisting me up. One hand stays there, his other arm banding around my back. He holds me as though my weight is nothing, those hazel eyes bright. "Remember – hold on."

He pushes into me gently, mindful of the solid steel lining his cock. I grip him, my face buried in the shirt he's still wearing as our hips bump together. He pumps in and out of me, slow enough that I shift, silently asking for me.

"Use your words."

"*Testa di cazzo*," I hiss, and Luciano Morelli *laughs* against my ear as he picks up the pace, his hips pistoning into me until my orgasm rolls over me in a sudden wave of sensation. I tighten around him – my arms, my pussy - as he follows me, pressing in as far as he can with a groan that rips from his throat. He holds me there for several seconds, his lips traveling against my neck before he slowly releases me and takes the towel Dante hands him.

My feet stumble, trying to catch their grip against the deck floor as he gently runs it over my sensitive skin, cleaning me off.

"Feeling a little off balance, *tentazione*?" Dante teases as he slips into Luc's vacated spot. I blindly reach behind me, feeling for the edge of the table. I feel full despite Luc's *very* thorough clean-up, swollen and thoroughly fucked already, and both Dante and Stefano are watching me with hungry gazes.

Slowly, I spread my legs. "Think you can steal the win, V'Arezzo?"

Dante's smirk is an echo of the boy he used to be, the boy that chased me until he caught me. Somehow, the man... he's even more devastating. "I'm not going to fuck you. Figured you could use the break."

I frown. "Oh."

Except he doesn't mean that. He can't, because he's unbuttoning his trousers, pulling out his cock as he runs his hand over it, tugging.

No. Instead, he crooks his finger. "Come here, *tentazione*."

Pursing my lips, I test my balance. Debate whether to risk it.

"Scared?"

My brows fly down. "Absolutely not."

I force my legs to straighten, force my face to settle into an aloof expression as I take those few steps away from the table. "See? I *told* you—,"

The world disappears from beneath my feet, along with every bit of breath from my body.

The blood rushes to my head as my vision orients itself, and I find myself face to face with Dante's cock. *Upside fucking down.* "What the fuck?"

He holds me tightly, arms around my back as my knees come to rest on his shoulders. "Wrap your arms around my waist, *tentazione*."

I take a breath, possibly to demand that he puts me the fuck *down*, except that at that precise moment, he buries his face in my pussy. Deep, long licks, teasing the swollen flesh, nipping at my clit.

I throw my arms out and around him, my eyes crossing. I almost feel dizzy with it, with the feeling of being upside down as he holds me steady and just... takes. The head of his cock is level with my lips as I lean forward, experimenting with a lick before I open my mouth and take him in.

He doesn't stop licking, doesn't break his concentration for a moment as I play with his cock, testing how far I can take him like this.

I get my answer when he hits the back of my throat, and I swallow.

Dante doesn't rush me, doesn't thrust – he just *holds* me, his arms a steady, solid band around my body as he licks me like a fucking ice-cream cone. Like this, it feels intense – I can't move, can't do anything but let him do exactly what he wants.

My thighs start to tremble around his head. Dante pushes his tongue inside me, mimicking a thrusting motion before he pulls out and clamps his lips over my clit, sucking.

My pussy flutters, squeezing desperately around empty air as my muscles contract. Dante's cock slips out of my mouth, and dizziness threatens.

My arms nearly slip. Dante has me upright in a moment, his movements steady as he rights us. His arms slide back around me as he keeps me upright.

I blink at him hazily as he pushes my hair back with a slight frown. "Dizzy?"

Dizzy, overloaded, full. I only blink at him hazily in response, and his hold on me tightens.

Just in time, as my legs crumple. He catches me with a curse, the others jumping to their feet. "I think you lost, Caterina."

Like fuck I did. The smirk I give him feels strange on my face. "You sure?"

Soft laughter from Luc. "Maybe we all won."

I blink, some of that haziness clearing. "Stefan?"

Warmth covers my bare back, his large hands landing on my shoulders. I'm still balancing against Dante, but he steps away, allowing

Stefan to wrap his arms around me as I lean back into him. He kisses my shoulder. "It's okay."

No, it's not. But my body stubbornly refuses to cooperate, and I glare at Dante. "You nearly broke me, *stronzo*."

He doesn't even look a little bit apologetic as he shrugs. "You loved every second of it."

Stefan pulls off the navy blazer he's wearing over his shirt, wrapping it around my shoulders. When he lifts me, I expect him to carry me to a seat.

But he places me down on the table instead, his blazer cushioning my back as I blink up at him. "When I said it was okay, I meant that I'll do all the work, Caterina. Lay back."

Oh.

I stretch out, listening to the sound of his zip. Stefan runs a finger up my center, pushing one inside, then another. He curves them, stroking against my walls as he watches. And my body slowly comes back to life beneath his soft, gentle touches. My hips begin to shift restlessly. "More."

"But you're tired." He pushes another finger inside me, one eyebrow raising cynically. "Perhaps we should stop."

"Do *not* stop." I push myself against him, my leg wrapping around his hip in an attempt to pull him closer. Stefan leans forward, careful not to place too much weight against the glass as he kisses me deeply.

And I gasp against his mouth, as the full length of his cock thrusts into me in one push. My hands wrap around his neck as he rocks into me, his pace slow and steady and enough to drive me out of my own mind, until I'm clawing at his back in silent demand. He grips my wrist, pushing it up.

"No." His smile is a curling, heated smirk that makes my stomach flip. "You're exhausted, Caterina. So lay back, and don't move."

He punctuates his words with a single, sharp thrust that makes my eyes cross.

My orgasm builds slowly as he works me into a pleading mess. But he doesn't stop, doesn't speed up. He tortures me with his patience until I'm dancing on the edge, my pussy fluttering around him. "I'm more than fucking awake now, damn you."

His teeth sink into my lower lip. "Good."

He pinches my clit hard, the shock of the touch enough to fucking catapult me off that cliff, my body twisting beneath Stefan as he fucks me through the waves until his hips twist and he groans against my lips.

I thump my head back against the glass, drinking in the stars. "So fucking good. Ten out of ten, Domenico."

"What?" Dante sounds furious. "Why does he get a ten?"

I wave my finger lazily. "For the date. Plan your own. I like this boat, though."

"It's a yacht," Luc murmurs. "And it happens to be yours, little crow. I even named it after you."

My eyes feel heavy, but I force them open. "Wow. Good game, Morelli. You can have an extra point."

And then I pass out.

CATERINA

Alessia is quiet this morning, no smiles as I carefully pick her up. Frowning, I walk over to the bed and settle on the edge. Behind me, the shower is running; the empty, mussed bedsheets telling me that Dante is already up.

My daughter looks up at me, her green eyes serious.

"Good morning," I whisper, running my hand over her curls and watching them bounce back into place. "What's the matter?"

I get no babbling conversation either. Instead, she slides her thumb into her mouth. "*Ba*."

As I study her tense expression, I wonder if she knows.

Today is the day we leave.

And in a rush, regret slams over me. I bend my head over hers, my lips pressed against her head as I breathe in the slight soapy scent that still lingers from the bath I clumsily gave her yesterday afternoon.

Behind me, a door opens and closes.

"You were right," I say quietly, not turning around.

We only regret the moments we don't have. And it tightens my throat, the thought of that time I spent when we first arrived keeping my distance.

I didn't want to hurt her. Hurt myself. But now, with our departure suddenly looming, I despise myself for it. Because what we have had isn't enough.

There's rustling behind me. Dante appears, a shirt hastily thrown on as he looks between us. He offers me a smile that fades when I don't return it. "I usually am. About what now?"

"The time I lost us." I shake my head. "How am I supposed to walk away from her again, Dante?"

She's been moved so *much*. She lost Bea, lost Pepe. Matteo took her, and Amie took care of her. And now I'm going to walk away and leave her behind.

He exhales. His fingers dance in front of Alessia's face, dropping away when she only watches him quietly, not grabbing for them. "You will not be away from her for long, Cat. Only as long as it takes, and we both know this will not be drawn out."

Matteo will not wait to move, once he knows we're back.

"Don't make a promise you can't keep."

"I'm not." His tone hardens. "I promise you, *tentazione*. You'll be back soon. You'll bring her home, and build on the foundations from this time. This time... it is not the only time. There will be more."

He sounds so certain. He presses a kiss to my lips, then to our daughter's head, before he stands. "Breakfast. Coffee. There is still time left. We're not running out of the door, Cat."

First, we wait.

Alessia, thankfully, brightens as we enter the kitchen. Her face lights up. "Ba!"

Stefano glances up with surprise. His eyes sweep across me, seeing too much. Or possibly remembering last night, judging by the way his lip curls into a small smile. I give him a tart look as I hand Alessia to him, and she immediately buries herself into the crook of his arm with an audibly happy sigh.

Dom, seated across from Stefan, leans forward, his voice coaxing. "Alessia."

She turns her head between them both, before she opens her arms for Dom. He grins as he plucks her from Stefan's lap. "Excellent taste."

The smile fades as she claps her arms and points straight back to Stefan.

Dante doesn't bother hiding his laughter as Gio walks in, his hair damp from a shower. "A new game, it seems."

Dom sighs, and I bite my cheek against my own smile as I lean against Luc's hip. He flips an omelet over. "Hungry?"

Not particularly. But I nod, pouring Gio and I a coffee as he presses a kiss to my cheek.

Breakfast is subdued. Alessia refuses to abandon her new game, so we get to watch Stefan and Dom work together to feed her scrambled eggs, yogurt and fruit in between passing her like a parcel as she laughs.

I scrunch up my nose at the yogurt. *Ugh.* I'm tempted to wash it out, but Alessia *loves* it. Instead, I pick at the omelet. "What time will your mother arrive?"

Luc sits back, fresh coffee in his hand. "Anytime. The pilot is on standby whenever we're ready."

My heart squeezes. "I'll go and pack, then."

Alessia looks up as I stand. "*Ma?*"

My heart. My fucking *heart*.

I hold out my arms. I expect her to turn away, back to her game, but she immediately reaches out her arms, and my stomach swoops as

I gather her up. She pats my cheek as I turn to leave, but my eyes catch on Dante.

He watches us both, not masking the strain on his face.

It's his last day with her too.

I tilt my head in silent invitation, and he's behind me in a second.

I set her down on the bed, and Dante settles down beside her. As I pack some of the things I've accumulated since I arrived, I listen to her steady stream of conversation, the rise and fall of her unintelligible words as Dante murmurs back to her. I drink every sound she makes in, holding it inside me and storing it.

I'm coming back for you.

We swap rooms, Dante packing his own bag as she crawls into my lap and starts to explore my hair. And my resolve hardens as I watch her.

I will not fail her again.

When Luc's voice echoes, Dante zips up the holdall. "Have you met his *madre* before?"

"No." I consider what I know. "He told me once that she was… loud. Protective."

And hopefully someone who won't mind a small houseguest for a while.

We hear her before we see her. A loud, irritated burst of Italian meets us as we head downstairs, Dante and I exchanging looks before they come into view.

Luc's mother has her son's hazel eyes. They narrow on him, her finger up and pointing as we come to a stop. She barely reaches his shoulders, dark haired and elegant, and he holds up his hands as she throws up her own. But he's smiling, a mixture of sadness and love in his face. "Ma*ma*."

She points at him again. "Do not *mama* me, Luciano Aurelio Morelli. I can still chase you around with my spoon. You should have come home sooner."

He agrees with a murmur, his arms wrapping around her. I catch her smile where he can't see before she buries it under a frown. But there are deep circles under her eyes, and I'm reminded that she recently lost her husband.

Loss, everywhere we look.

She wipes down her hands before turning to us, shooting Luc an expectant look.

He clears his throat.

"Mama," he waves a hand. "This is Dante V'Arezzo. And... Caterina Corvo. This is my *madre*, Lucia Morelli."

She looks me up and down. "Your Caterina?"

I suddenly wonder with a flush exactly what Luc has told his mother about me. "*Buongiorno, signora*. Thank you for having us in your home."

Luc smirks at Dante. "Sì. *My* Cat."

Dante's look in his direction can only be described as withering, but he leans in to kiss Lucia on both cheeks. "*Grazie, signora*. Your home is beautiful."

She waves him off, and I stiffen as she moves to me. She eyes me with intent – as if I'm being judged.

And then she smiles. "Benvenuto, Caterina Corvo. My son speaks of you... *often*."

Luc groans behind her at the teasing words, and I grin back at her as she turns back to Dante. To Alessia in his arms.

Lucia Morelli's smile grows. "And you, *piccola*, you must be Alessia. You and I are to be excellent friends, I hear."

Alessia takes her offered finger, waving it around. Lucia turns back to me, linking our arms together. She snaps her fingers at Luc, waving him away.

"Coffee, Luciano. I brought Alonso back with me, he'll get my bags. You will gift your mother a conversation before you run away and leave me. Take the charming one with you."

Both Dante and Luc start. I eye them, but they wither under Lucia's expectant look, disappearing into the kitchen.

Nothing sends the fear of God into the men of the Cosa Nostra quite like their mothers.

I brace, but she only squeezes my hand. "It is hard to leave a child behind."

Straight to the point. "I—,"

"She will be here," Lucia says gently. "Whenever you are ready, and it is safe. The staff will very much enjoy spoiling her, as will I. As a *nipotina*. It has been a long time since we had children in the house."

Littlest granddaughter.

My eyes start to burn, and she pats my cheek. "My Luciano has a big heart, Caterina Corvo. Do not break it."

There's steel there beneath her words, and I shake my head. "Never."

The others appear behind us as we enter the kitchen, and Luc introduces them to an impassive Lucia. There's amusement there as she inspects them. "Quite a collection of friends you have, Luciano. And all very handsome."

She winks at me as every single one of them flushes crimson. "Lucky girl."

There's no judgment on our unusual set-up. Despite demanding that Luc make coffee, Lucia pushes him into a chair and efficiently seizes control of the kitchen, tossing dozens of questions at us and somehow pulling together endless plates of food along the way. Alessia chews on a soft oatmeal cookie in Stefan's arms, and Lucia cocks her head.

"*You*. You are quiet, no?"

He pales.

Her voice softens. "You will introduce me to your mamma after lunch. Sì?"

"*Sì* – of course. *Grazie*, *sig-* uh, Lucia."

She nods, satisfied. I glance around.

None of us have a mother like this. Perhaps Gio did, once, and Stefan, with Iliana. Dom lost his parents as a child, Bea stepping in to fill the role. I never knew my mother. Dante doesn't remember his.

I wonder if she knows that, as she fills our plates with food and drags personal information about our likes and dislikes from us without batting an eye. Perhaps she knew them, or some. Something tells me she did, and Lucia Morelli has decided to take us under her wing.

Starting with food.

As we get up to finalize our leaving arrangements, she's already packing food into containers as Stefan lingers uncertainly, muttering about *airplane food* and *poison*.

Luc stops Dante and I on the stairs. "Are you comfortable? Leaving Alessia here?"

Dante looks at me. "It's your decision."

"I am. Your mother is a force of nature," I admit. "I like her, Luc."

He cups my cheek. "And she likes you. I think. But probably not as much as she seems to like Alessia. She adores her already."

I think I'm perfectly fine with that.

Dante

"Cat."

My chest hurts as I say her name. My voice is low, quiet in the dark room. "*Tentazione*. It's time."

She doesn't move. She stays where she is at the edge of Alessia's crib. Gio and I moved it into Lucia's bedroom under her watchful eye an hour ago.

Slowly, I move up to stand beside her. It feels as if a cord stretches directly from my heart to the little girl sleeping in her arms, her small hand curled up above her head. I rocked her myself, back and forth, until her eyes fluttered closed before I relinquished her to Cat.

And now she stands, deathly still, her eyes bright.

I considered asking her to stay, as I handed Alessia over. For a second – for a moment. Cat would be safe, and Alessia would at least have one of us.

But... that's not who she is. And if we lose, they would still track her down. Matteo Corvo would never leave Caterina Corvo as a risk.

"You will see her again." I stroke my hand over those wild curls, one more time. "I made you a promise."

I intend to keep it.

At the soft knock on the door, we both turn. Gio offers us an apologetic grimace. "I'm sorry. But... I just had a call from Johnno."

Both of us go still. Our time is up.

We can't keep the world out any longer.

Cat lets out a long, trembling breath, before she places Alessia in the crib, tugging the light blanket over her. A moment passes, two, as we wait silently before she straightens.

She doesn't look back.

I try, try not to torture myself, but I can't help it. Hades himself could not stop me from looking over my shoulder, drinking the sight of my daughter in.

And then I follow.

Farewells are already happening in the entrance hall. Our luggage has been loaded into the cars, and as we walk down Luc wraps his mother in a tight embrace. "We'll be back soon."

Her eyes travel over all of us when he steps back. Lucia Morelli knows what we're walking into.

But it's Cat that she speaks to. "Take care of my son. Please."

Cat's throat bobs as she nods. "And you will take care of Alessia."

Lucia hugs her, whispering something in her ear that smooths away the worried lines around her eyes.

Stefano jogs down after us. "Ready."

Cat follows Stefano and Dom to one car. Luc, Gio and I get in the other, none of us speaking as we pull away from the house.

That cord tugs on my chest. Harder, sharper, straining until it feels as though it snaps completely as we move out of sight. As though I'm missing a piece of me.

A hand grips my shoulder. "She'll be absolutely ruined by the time we get back. My mother adores children."

I clear my throat, trying to find the words. Gio's phone rings, and we glance over as he answers it. "Johnno."

He listens, a frown appearing and deepening between his eyes. He puts the call on speaker. "Say that again."

"*Cops.*" Johnno sounds strained. "Dozens of them, Gio. We picked them up on a camera we left behind, just in case."

"Behind where?" Luc straightens beside me.

"The Asante compound." Johnno sounds grim. "It's not a completely clean site, not yet. We had fires burning for two days before we could even send the first cleaning team. We watched them for a few hours, hoping they'd fuck off. But they've put a damn cordon up."

Fuck.

Luc is already pulling up his phone, dialing. Stefano answers on the first ring. "What is it?"

Luc's voice is clipped as he explains. Cat's voice comes over the intercom, sounding livid. "There were hundreds of people in that compound every day. None of us are in the system. They have no reason to look in our direction – not to mention they know fucking *better*."

We pay them enough to look away.

"I'm in the system."

We all stop at Stefano's short words. "I was an asshole teenager. Salvatore left it on my record."

"Doesn't matter," I say finally. "Cat is right. Someone not in our pocket caught wind of a fire and poked their noses in. This is nothing we can't sort out."

"Or someone pointed them in our direction." Pure ice coats Cat's words. "Someone who'd like to see us dead – or in for twenty to life. Care to bet on who?"

"You think Matteo broke omertà?"

"You *don't*?" She sounds disbelieving. "Of course he did. He saw an opportunity to pin us and took it. Like Dante said, it's nothing we can't sort out, but it will slow us down and that's the last thing we need. We need their eyes away from us, or we're sitting fucking *ducks*."

I scrub my hand over my face. Gio leans over the phone, Luc holding his out so they can all hear.

Dom speaks next. "If he's trying to pin what happened at the Asante compound on someone, pushing the cops in that direction, it's a shot in the dark at best. Stefano, you're most likely to catch the heat for it if your prints come up on a search."

"Stay here," Cat says immediately. "We can work on it – fix it before it becomes an issue."

"No." His voice is hard. "I go where you go."

"Stefan—,"

"Not a discussion," he says shortly. "I'm not leaving your side, Cat. If they come after me, we'll find a way out of it."

"Johnno," Gio says. "Keep a watch on the house. If they leave it, or security is light, get in there and make sure they don't find a fucking thing."

"Sure, boss."

"Take Rocco with you." I glance down, my fingers flying across the screen as I message him. My enforcer can move faster than anyone I've met. If he doesn't want to be seen, he won't be.

"No problem, Dante."

Gio gives me a hard stare as the call ends. "Tell me *my* damn enforcer didn't just take an order from you."

"*Enough.*" Dom sounds frustrated. "We all know this is most likely to be a trap for Cat. She's the one he wants."

"Don't even ask." Her voice is hard. "We'll manage it, Domenico."

Caterina

I slip into the small bedroom about an hour before we land, unzipping the holdall and laying the clothes out on the bed.

Stripping out of the linen trousers, the white camisole that's better suited for the Sicilian sun, I change into the supple black leather trousers, pulling them up and over my waist. The scarlet red blouse – one of my favorites – goes on next, the deep v-neck showing only a hint of my scar when I move. The edge of the ruined crow's wings stand out more clearly at this angle.

The black heels follow, red soles flashing as I slide my feet into them before tugging my hair into a tight, high ponytail.

Ducking into the bathroom, I apply my make-up. A precise flick of eyeliner. My lips are lined perfectly, filled with a deep red.

Layer by layer, I put myself back together. And when I look at my reflection, I could almost kid myself that the last few months haven't happened at all.

I stop when I walk out of the bathroom.

"I thought you might want them," Gio says carefully. He holds up my knives with a nod at my shoes. "So I asked Vincent to send them. I packed them, though. Before we came for you."

I blow out a breath. "I feel more like myself, at least. Thank you."

More prepared to face whatever is coming for us when we land.

Gio hands me the knives, watching as I select the two daggers Luc gave me, sliding them into the back of my shoes. "If he *has* broken Omertà, he's handed you a heavy advantage."

"I know." I already mapped it, Dom and Stefano feeding in on the drive to the private airfield. "None of the men will willingly follow him if he has."

Aside from my uncle's men, nobody has stepped forward as an ally. But if they're waiting, testing the waters, this could be the ammunition I need to push them into my corner.

"I suppose we'll find out."

I emerge from the bedroom and settle into the seat beside Dom. His jaw is tight. "I don't agree with this."

"Tough." I don't look at him. "I made the call."

He turns his phone over in his hand. "I tried to call Vincent for back-up, but he's not answering. Nor Tony."

And he sounds *pissed*. "I've been out of the loop for too fucking long, Cat."

"You and me both. It'll be easier than you think to fall back into it, Dom. We've spent years doing this. Our whole lives preparing for it. A few months don't take away years of work."

He grimaces. "Is your uncle still on campus?"

I check my phone. "I don't know."

And I forgot to ask Vincent for his number. Stupid, careless mistakes.

I can't afford to make any, small or large.

The pilot's voice filters over the intercom. "Landing. Please take your seats."

We land with a bump, the plane hurtling over the tarmac. We're all out of our seats before it stops.

"Fuck." Luc swings his head between Stefano and me. "You were right."

I press my lips together. "Maybe."

"They look like cops to me," Gio says grimly. "This isn't good."

Three cars pull up beside the plane, lights flashing. "Give me your gun."

Dante stares at me incredulously as Gio immediately pulls out his Glock, handing it to me. I take it with a nod, gesture at Dante. "I need another. *Now*, Dante."

He shakes his head. "You can't be serious. You start a shootout here and we're all dead, Cat. They'll turn a blind eye to a lot, but you won't walk out alive."

"I'm not starting anything." I stride up to him, my hand sliding into his holster and pulling out a pistol. I flick the safety on, shoving it into the back of my trousers with a wince. Never the best idea.

They follow as I dart to the bedroom. Luc starts pulling off his own weapons, handing them to Stefano. Quickly, I pull two smaller pins from my dagger set, winding my hair into a bun and sticking them in. "Any pens on this plane?"

"Cat." Dom's brows dip. "What the hell are you doing?"

I shove past him. "Why *would* Matteo break omertà now? It makes no fucking sense – he knows he'd lose the entire Cosa Nostra, whatever he chooses to call himself."

"Because he's a psychopath," Dom snaps. "And he wants you dead."

"Exactly." I yank open drawers until I find a biro, snapping off the plastic piece and shoving it into my shoe. Another piece goes into my bra, digging into my skin. "But he wants to *watch*, Dom. He doesn't want me locked up, getting out and coming after him."

"It's a set-up," Luc breathes in understanding. "You think it's fake?"

I nod. "Call Johnno. Ask him how many cops are covering the Asante compound right now."

Stefan glances out of the window. "There's a whole lot of fucking guns out there either way, Cat. We don't have long."

Gio mutters into the phone before he looks up. "*One.*"

I finally stop, my hands running over the blatant, visible weapons strapped to me. "We burned more than eighty bodies that night. There's a fucking *human trafficking* set-up in the basement. You think if they were really paying attention, they'd leave *one* cop watching over all of that?"

A tic appears in Dom's jaw. "You think he's going to separate you from us."

I nod. "A fake arrest, and I'm away in the car. He'll probably leave you alive, let it play out, just to pander to his warped fucking brain. I get delivered to Matteo, and he gets to rub his clever little plan in *my* face. You wouldn't even know until you tried to find me, and he'd watch you tie yourselves up in knots when there's no record of my arrest at all."

I can only imagine his delight over the details of this one.

"*Probably* leave us alive," Gio mutters. "So what is the plan?"

Squaring my shoulders, I face them. "I'm going to leave with them."

"Like *fuck* you are," Dom says immediately.

Four equally vehement refusals ring out. All except for Luc. He stares at the floor, frowning. I wave off their protests. "They'll search me for weapons. They'll find some, not all. They won't be expecting me to fight back. It's an easy win."

"In a *moving car*," Luc says quietly. "They could easily take the upper hand, Cat. Knock you out. Drug you. And you would be *gone*."

My heart thumps at the pain in his words. "I'm not going to let that happen again, Luc. And we don't have many options. There's more of them out there than there are of us."

More guns.

Everything – the lives of the men in front of me – hinges on what I know of Matteo, and the way he operates.

"He wants to cause as much pain as possible," I say, my throat tight. "He kills me first. Then pushes in and hits the rest of you."

"You're asking us to gamble your life on this," Dante says heavily.

But I hold his gaze. "I could have kept quiet and gone with them anyway."

But I promised him. And he closes his eyes. "Alright."

"No." Dom pushes in front of me, his hands on my shoulders. "*No*."

"I'm giving you an order, Dom." He jerks as if I've slapped him. "Are you my enforcer, or not? Am I your capo, or *not*?"

Gio stirs. "We have to make it look real. *Without* them suspecting. If they suspect, if they think we're going to fight, they'll just shoot anyway."

"Can you do it?" I ask Dom outright. "If not, tell me now, Domenico."

He grits his teeth. "Fine."

I toss my phone to Luc. "Follow as soon as you can. Check the sides of the road."

Stefan murmurs something to Dom as I pass them, striding to the exit. The stairs are in place, a handful of terrified-looking staff huddled together on the ground below us as they watch the *cops*.

"I'll see you in a few minutes," I say softly, glancing over my shoulder. "And you'd better come after me. If any of you get shot, I'm going to be *really* fucked off."

With that, I rip the door open.

Shouting erupts immediately. I emerge slowly, my hands above my head as guns point in our direction. Men duck behind car doors, the glint of barrels focusing on each of us as they follow me down.

A woman strides toward us, clad in a sleek navy-blue suit. Her eyes sweep over me. "Caterina Asante?"

I barely stop myself from flinching as I offer her a cool, unimpressed look. "It's Corvo. How can we be of assistance, Officer...?"

"Rankin." She holds up an ID badge, snapping it closed before sliding it into her pocket. I note the gun hanging from her left side. "May I ask where your husband is at the moment?"

"Abroad." I wave a hand. "You know what these businessmen can be like."

She eyes the men behind me. "Keep your hands in the air. All of you."

I feign irritation. "Am I in some sort of trouble? I have an excellent relationship with the Police Commissioner. I can call him now – I'm sure he can sort this out quickly."

"I'm with RICO." She moves behind me. "Caterina Asante, I'm arresting you on suspicion of murder and human trafficking. You have the right to remain silent. Anything you say can and will be used against you in a court of law. You have the right to an attorney, and if you do not have one, one will be appointed for you."

There's derision in her tone. "I'm sure that won't be a problem, though, for a rich bitch like you."

Ouch.

She pats me down, pulling out the guns Dante and Gio gave me and tossing them aside. An argument breaks out behind me, cops spreading out to separate me from the men demanding more information, feigning outrage as guns are shoved in their faces. "What about them?"

She turns me, slapping a pair of cuffs around my wrist and tightening them. "Just you. The guns are a precaution, given your... background."

I smile. "I should think you'd be a little more careful of insulting me, then. As you say – given my *background*. I'll be out within a few hours. You'll find that I have a lot of friends in law enforcement, Officer Rankin."

She leans in. This woman hates me, for whatever reason. I can see it in her eyes, in the filthy look she gives me. "Where *you're* going, your background won't matter. I can promise you that."

Bingo.

I open my mouth, but a shout carries over the row happening behind us. We both turn, the metal cuffs already cutting into my wrists.

Stefan.

The men gripping his arms struggle to contain him as he surges forward until we can make out his words. "I killed Salvatore Asante."

My heart stops. "*Stefan—*,"

Behind him, the others stop. Gio, Dante and Luc all look between us, wariness on their faces. Only Dom doesn't move. Instead, he meets my stare with his chin lifted.

Stefan doesn't look at me. Instead, he stares straight at Rankin. "I killed him. I can give you details, as much as you need."

I clamp my mouth shut. Rankin stares between us, her brows dipping. "Fine. Two for one then. Cuff him."

He holds his hands out silently, and then we're both being pulled, tugged to the waiting car that idles a few feet away. Rankin pushes me into the back, behind the driver. Stefan joins me on the other side.

"Go," Rankin says sharply. Wheels screech as we pull away, leaving them behind.

I sit facing straight ahead, only my eyes moving as I look around. My voice is a low hiss. "What the hell are you *doing*?"

"Where you go, I go." There's not an ounce of regret in his voice as he studies the plastic screen separating us from the front. "Whatever happens."

I don't know whether to kiss him or punch him. A problem to consider – later.

Slowly, my eyes lingering on Rankin, I lean forward. Her search was sloppy at best, and the shim I created from the broken pen lid slides easily into my hand. Rankin is muttering into her phone, and I pause when her eyes dart up to the rearview mirror.

As soon as she looks away, my hand fiddles with the shim, sliding it into the locking mechanism. It takes a few seconds before I'm able to get it into place and push the cuffs down, tightening them with a silent prayer.

They click open. Breathing deeply, I pass the shim to Stefan and slide my knives from the back of my heels.

Fucking *idiots*.

After his own cuffs click free, I hand him one of my knives before dropping the other in my lap. Keeping my wrists pushed together, I lift my hands and prod experimentally at the plastic that separates us from the front. It moves beneath my fingers, a poor imitation of what you'd see in a real cop car.

I'm almost disappointed.

Stefan taps my knee, his gazes questioning. I move my hands to show him, nodding at his own area. My lips move. *On three.*

One.

Two.

"Hey, Rankin," I call through the plastic. She glances back at me with a smug smile. "How much is Matteo paying you?"

The smile slides off her face, but mine grows.

"*Three.*"

I pull my hand back and slam it into the plastic as hard as I can. It parts like butter beneath the lethally sharp edge of my dagger – straight into the neck of the driver. Beside me, Stefan's jab is vicious enough to pop the screen out of its weak fastening, even as the dagger goes straight through Rankin's throat.

The car swerves, veers wildly to the side. "*Shit—.*"

Stefan pulls his dagger free, his hand grabbing for the door as wet, gurgling sounds come from the seats in front of us. Breathing hard, I yank the dagger in my hand as far as I can to the left, praying that it shifts the driver's weight.

It works a little too well.

I slam against the door, Stefan almost sliding into me as the car spins. His eyes meet mine, full of fear as he throws his arm across my chest.

Neither of us is wearing a *belt*—

Metal crumples around us with a screeching sound as the world flips. My head slams into the roof as I'm flung into the air, Stefan's arm catching me before it gets ripped away.

I try to suck air into my lungs as the car rocks, and then settles on its roof. A hissing noise sounds as I blink the dizziness away. The taste of iron floods my mouth. "Ste... Stefan."

My hand bangs against the window. Again. I twist my head, ignoring the burst of pain. "Stefan?"

Voices, panicked voices, calling my name. Stefan's name. Groggy, I reach for his shoulder, shake it. "They're here. It worked."

He's still silent, and icy tendrils begin to wrap around my chest. "*Stefano.*"

Sharper this time, tinged with panic. His face is turned away from me, and why the fuck isn't he *saying* anything—

Faces at the window, banging on it. Ignoring them, I pull myself over to him, turn his face to mine. His dark eyes are hidden beneath closed eyelids, and I wipe at the blood on his face.

He looks like he's sleeping—

Glass smashes behind me. "Cat. Are you hurt?"

"Help him," I rasp. "Dom. Help him."

"Talk to me—,"

"*Help him!*"

I scream the words around a raw throat.

More glass. And then Dom's face appears on my other side beside Stefan, his eyes sweeping over me, over Stefano. He stills. "Dante!"

There are hands on me from the other side, and I struggle against Luc as he drags me out. There are tears on my face as he grips my cheeks, turns my head back and forth. "Are you hurt?"

"*Stefan—,*"

"They're getting him." He's pale. "*Merda*, Cat, when I saw the car flip—,"

"I'm okay," I say through numb lips. But I'm not.

He has to wake up.

I pull out of Luc's arms, darting around the car. They're lifting him out, and I step back to give them space. Dom presses his fingers against Stefan's neck. "He's breathing, Cat."

My knees couldn't hold me up if I tried. I crash down beside him, leaning over to check for myself as the buzzing in my head begins to recede. "Just knocked out?"

Dom nods. "Looks that way. What about you?"

I glance down, making a brief assessment before dismissing the light cuts. "I'm fine."

"For the record, this was *not* one of your better plans."

Beneath my hands, Stefan coughs. His eyes open slowly, pupils wide as he starts to struggle. Dom pushes him back down. "Steady. Take a minute."

His eyes dart around before they land on me. "You hurt?"

My mouth feels dry as I shake my head. Luc's hand lands on my shoulder. "Your phone is ringing."

I glance down at Vincent's name, my voice hoarse as I pick up. "Yeah."

Frowning, I try to hear him over the noise in the background. "What?"

My entire body goes cold. "We're coming."

Dom is pulling Stefan to his feet, helping him find his balance. "What's happened?"

But it's Luc that I turn to. "Matteo has pulled his men from the campus. We need to get back, *now*."

Domenico

I stare out of the window as we pass through the campus gates.

Home.

It's been months since I was last here. And I expect to feel out of place, as if everyone here carried on as normal while we were going through hell. As if I no longer fit here at all.

Instead, it looks... neglected.

The shrubbery, the neat bushes and trees that normally line the road in immaculately maintained lines is overgrown and browning, branches brushing against the car as we pass. I don't see a single person, not a single sign of life anywhere as Gio pulls into the parking lot.

But a heaviness lingers in the air. As if we're entering a ghost town.

My hand slips down to check my gun as Cat does the same, perched on my lap. I can tell she feels it too, her brown eyes lost in thought and grief as she wipes over her daggers again.

This is not the same place we left. That much is clear as the doors slam behind us and we make our way down the path, toward the Courtyard.

Cat throws her shoulders back and strides ahead. Luc walks beside her, his jaw tight with anger. Gio and Dante fall into place on either side of them, a half-step behind.

The message sent is not for them. But they're a sight nonetheless, the four of them striding onto campus together after months of separation.

Only Stefano stays back, silently walking next to me. Dried blood still cakes his skin from the glass as he scrubs at it with his hand.

"Thanks," I say tightly. He turns to look at me. "For going with her."

"I meant what I said." His words are low enough so the others can't hear. "I'm not leaving her. Unless she tells me to, and probably not even then. A lifetime is a long time to be your enemy, Domenico."

I know that feeling. All too well. "You're not my enemy."

Perhaps he might have been. But there was no lie in Cat's petrified face when she thought she had lost him.

Cat comes to a stop, turning. "Stefan."

It's not a request. He steps forward, Gio standing aside to make space between him and Luc.

A message. The five heirs – now capos - of the Cosa Nostra.

United and strong.

"Domenico."

I jerk my head to Cat. There's a slight smile on her face as she tilts her head. Dante is already shifting, leaving a space between them on her right as he nods at me.

Ignoring the tightening of my throat, I walk up to them and take the place she offers me.

"So." Luc turns to face forward, his mouth a tight line. "Let's see what he's left us to work with."

Luciano

The Courtyard is full.

Although I wouldn't call it a crowd.

Pockets of people linger in small groups. Corvo, Morelli, V'Arezzo, Fusco, even a handful of Asante students. They whisper to each other as they back away to let us through, their eyes lingering on Cat. On all of us.

She chose our entrance well.

But there are not enough here. Not nearly enough, and by the tightening of Cat's face, she realizes it too.

This is no army.

Too young, too raw.

Too scared.

And these are the ones who chose to stay.

Our enforcers are waiting beside the red oak tree. Shadows from the weight swinging from the branches next to them darken Nico's face as he steps forward. "I'm fucking glad to see you, Luc."

"Likewise." Vincent has his head bent, murmuring to Cat as Rocco and Dante listen in. "Have you looked?"

He shakes his head, his mouth pressed into a grim line. "You said not to."

I did. The message is mine. I won't let anyone else carry the nightmare of whatever is waiting for me.

I turn to the oak tree – one part of this campus that does look untouched. The red leaves glisten like freshly spilled blood, and I sweep my eyes over the gift Matteo has left me.

Three bodies hang from the branches, swaying lightly in the breeze and covered in thick black plastic.

Three dark hoods cover their faces.

Cat stays by my side as I reach out and rip a white envelope from the middle body. My name is printed on the outside in sprawling, messy handwriting.

Luciano,

I know how much you enjoy a party.

- MC

"That's it?" Cat frowns.

I flip the note over. Written on the other side is a date and time.

"Two hours from now," Cat mutters. "Any bet this is connected to his little RICO game?"

"I wouldn't waste my money." Slowly, I reach for the first hood on the left, tugging it off.

The mannequin spins slowly, grotesquely painted in the mockery of a face. "The hell is *that* supposed to be?"

Cat slides a knife free. She stabs it into the plastic, slicing through the thick material and ripping it away.

The bottom drops out of my stomach as I take in the thick black letters printed across the mannequin's chest.

AMIE.

I stare at those letters for more than a minute before I crumple the note in my hand, storming over to the swaying figure on the right and rip the hood away.

Another mannequin.

Cat's face turns ashen. "*Vincent.*"

At her shout, he appears beside her, Dom a half-step behind him. "Where's Tony?"

Vincent hesitates. "I don't know. He hasn't been around much."

"Call him," she says tightly. "Right now. Tell him to get back here within the hour."

Vincent follows her eyes, curses as he digs in his pocket. Frowning, I look between them and back to the mannequin, taking in the jagged mark slashed down its face. I don't recognise it, twisted as it is. "Who is this supposed to be?"

Silently, she slices the plastic away, and behind me, both Gio and Stefano hiss in realization.

FRANKIE.

Stefano steps around me, moving for Cat, but she ducks away from him, holding up a hand. "Don't."

"It's not your fault." He pushes those words at her, even as the guilt crawls across her face.

"She went there for me that night," she says tightly. "And she didn't come out. Salvatore found her."

I think of the women dancing around Matteo, night after night. The boasts he made of his alliance with Salvatore Asante. His *regular supply*. "And he gave her to Matteo."

Gio sounds rough when he speaks. "She knew the risks, Cat. She chose to go. She wanted to fight."

Cat stares down at her nails, searching for something. I don't stop her when she stalks to the final mannequin and rips off the hood.

It slips from her hand, her lips parting as she jerks back.

The boy is almost unrecognizable. The flesh has been ripped away, torn and hacked to leave little more than a lump of flesh behind, fleshless lips twisted in a horrific, final scream. Swallowing, Cat steps closer to examine him. "It's... it's Alessandro."

Beside me, Dom swipes his hand over his face. "Fucking hell. He was barely more than a *kid*."

Cat is staring at those sightless eyes, her muscles locked. She doesn't argue when I take the dagger from her hand and rip through the final piece of material. The name has been carved into his battered chest in spiky scarlet letters.

CATERINA.

She remains still. "Sandro was the hacker I sent into the Corvo accounts."

The hacker that locked Matteo out.

"Two hours," I say quietly. An apology in my voice. "It's not much time to prepare."

"No. But we have had longer than that," she says tightly. She gestures for the knife, flipping the handle in her hand as she looks up at the rope holding Alessandro's body off the ground. And then she throws it, the roar of rage tearing from her throat as the knife slices through. She catches him without flinching, grips him and lowers him to the floor before kneeling. Her head bows.

Dom's hand on my arm stops me. "Give her a minute."

I turn, taking in the avid onlookers. Some of them inch closer, craning to see. When I cross my arms, Dom turns too. Gio follows. Dante. Stefano.

They decide to look away and fucking fast.

Caterina

Sixty seconds.

That's all I give myself. All I can give Sandro, before I stand.

My men have their backs to me. The Courtyard is almost empty now, and I play with the knife in my hand.

Amie.

Frankie.

And me.

Three bodies planned for. Three nooses.

"Gather as many as you can," I say tightly. "Anyone who can provide cover fire, but they need good aim. We need to be able to fire as many bullets as possible, as *quickly* as possible, in a rolling wave without breaks."

Dom gives me a questioning look. "We don't have automatic weapons here."

"Glock switches," Stefan's brows draw down. "Attach them to a handgun and it turns into a semi-automatic."

I look at the nooses again. The names. "Get them. And as many Glocks as you can dig up. We need someone fast, too. Several of them. And strong."

"Rocco," Dante says immediately. Cat nods. "Who else?"

"Tony." Vincent's grief is clear, his voice guttural. "He's coming."

"Anyone else?" Luc asks, but I shake my head.

I can see his desperation, his guilt. It hovers inside my own chest, too. "Luc – the chances of us actually getting them out of there – it's slim. Slim to none."

Frankie and Amie might die today. They might even be dead already, but as I look back at those nooses, I doubt it.

Because the third noose is mine. I wonder if Matteo has realized yet that his little lap dog will not be delivering me as planned. That his grand finale will be missing the guest of honor.

I glance over at Dante, at Gio. Dante notices my stare first. "What does that look mean?"

I remember how steady he was as I ran for him the night of the battle. How the bullets missed my head by millimeters at most, his grip not wavering as he held off the wave of Asante men hunting me down. How Gio took over, both of them perfect with their aim.

But this – they'll have a split second. Less, maybe.

To save a life. Or to take one.

Caterina

I don't recognise my childhood home.

There is filth *everywhere*. Broken glass crunches under our feet as we walk up the drive, the scent of bleach and something more putrid digging into my nose. Decaying.

Dom's arm brushes against mine, and I look at him.

He spent months here, in this hellhole. *Months*, watching this. Living with it every day, tied to Matteo's side.

And now, his face is dark as he walks back toward it.

The music is no surprise. There's no bass, only a low melody that floats from the smashed windows. And on the balcony wrapping around the first floor, the balcony I was never allowed on as a child, my cousin waits for us.

My eyes sweep the space around him. There's no sign of Amie or Frankie, but the three pieces of rope attached to the railings make my throat tighten, as if I can *feel* those nooses tightening around my neck.

"Weapons up."

My quiet words are repeated back row by row, the several dozen soldiers with us lifting their weapons and training them on the man who grins, his arms spreading out in welcome. Others around him begin to turn, drinks in their hands.

I don't wait for him to spout whatever bullshit he's prepared, calling up. "You're becoming predictable, Matteo."

My raised voice carries across the space between us. The music cuts out, and a flicker of darkness edges into his grin. "Is that so?"

"It seems that I'm late to my own party." I gesture to the middle piece of rope. It's the only one hanging over the edge, the noose swaying. "Asphyxiation has never been my idea of fun, I'm afraid."

Matteo looks around, taking in the men gathered around me. His lip curls at Domenico. "I see your lap dog has crawled back to you. A little more battered than before. Has he told you his body count, *cugina*? I'm surprised you'd allow a mutt like him into your ranks. He has more blood on his hands than I do."

I tilt my head, fighting to keep my expression cool even as Dom tenses beside me. "You only butcher the innocent. *Coward*."

I step forward. Away from the protective line of my men. "You are a *coward*. Too weak. Too frightened to face me one-on-one. No - you'd prefer to play your little games, to lie and deceive and hide behind the walls of that house with your parties. Although I notice they're looking a little smaller now, since you lost access to the Corvo accounts. Where are all your men that protect you, Matteo? Have they lost interest, now that you're no longer *paying* them?"

His face twists with rage. "Still here, I'm afraid. You may have enjoyed your little hacking trick, but there are plenty of assets in this house. I am the Corvo capo, after all. I have plenty of allies, Caterina. Perhaps I'll give you to another one when I'm done with you. Your leash seems to have slipped."

I throw my head back, and I *laugh* through the ice in my stomach, laughing up at him. "You're welcome to try. If you can find one, that is. Considering what I did to the last man who thought he could control me. Do you know what I did to him? What part of him I *cut off*?"

My eyes slide to the few men still lingering on the balcony. One or two quietly move out of sight.

My voice is hard. Strong. "And as for *you* – oh, I have plans for you, cousin. I am finished playing your pathetic little games. You have shamed the Corvo name. You shame the Cosa Nostra, everything we stand for, and I am fucking tired of it. So be a good boy and send my people out, before I decide to *come in and get them.*"

I smirk up at his stony face. Pray that he doesn't call my bluff, that he truly is the coward I know him to be.

I slide my hand into the pockets of my trousers, and I wait.

Come on, asshole. Don't disappoint me now.

You wanted to play. Let's play.

Matteo's hands clench against the railing as if he's imagining my neck beneath his hands. His skin mottles with anger, spittle collecting at the corner of his mouth as his hideous caps gleam. "You want them back, I'm only too happy to give them to you."

I force my feet to stay still as they appear on either side of him, their arms tightly gripped.

A low noise sounds from a few feet along from me, and I glance back. Tony shifts, Vincent murmuring to him as he puts his hand on his chest to stop him pushing forward.

Frankie stands tall, her chin lifted. Some bruising litters her face, but she stands on her own two feet.

My eyes shift to Amie. And behind me, a low, guttural groan tears from Luc's throat.

I'm not even certain that it's her at first. So much *blood* covers her face, savage, deep cuts over every part of her exposed skin. She slumps against the men holding her, not able to hold herself up. Unconscious, or close to. Her eyes barely open beneath the swelling, fresh wounds on top of old.

And her *hair* – the hair she was always so proud of, vain about – her hair is gone. Hacked off in clumps, scant patches of blond dotted over a scalp riddled with fucking *burns*.

"Jesus," someone breathes. Rocco.

This plan – as long a shot as it always was, has now become even harder. Because Amie looks as though she's in her final moments, as if they have pushed her to the edge just in time for us to witness it.

Matteo doesn't say a thing. He just watches, grinning.

I have had my fill of men like him. Of men like Matteo, and Salvatore, who see us as things for them to own and control and hurt – as less than them, *belonging* to them.

I am so fucking tired, as I stare at Amie's face. Tired of failing. Of my own self-loathing, of seeing the same nightmares, night after night. But I will have to live with those memories, because of *them*. Amie and Frankie will have to live with it, too.

But first, they have to *live*.

"Choose," Matteo calls, his voice light and amused again. "One lives. One dies. Or possibly both, since you've managed to irritate me, cousin. I had to change the game, since you weren't here. I'm not feeling in an overly *giving* mood. But you won't know either way, not until you decide."

I breathe in as the nooses are wrapped around their necks, the knot tightened. Frankie doesn't move, doesn't look down at us. At Tony, as he surges forward with an agonized plea. "*Cat, please.*"

They're shoved to the edge of the railings, their feet pushed over.

Vincent pulls him back as I watch. Slowly, I slide out my gun, testing. Around me, the others do the same.

Men flood out onto the balcony, each of them with their own weapons. Dozens of them, all pointed at us. Two sides with guns raised watch each other.

"You see," Matteo murmurs. "Some of this artwork is worth a lot of money, Caterina. More than enough to pay the bills until that little inconvenience is fixed. So we have a stalemate."

I ignore him as Amie stirs. Her eyes open a little more. I'm not sure if she can even see me before they close again.

We're running out of time.

"So?" Matteo yawns. "I'm a busy man. I have an empire to run, *cugina*, so get on with it."

Slipping the gun back into my holster, I pull out my dagger instead. Twirl it in my hands, and shrug. "I don't particularly care. Kill them both."

"*No.*" Tony roars at me, and there is no feigning the terror in his voice despite the discussion we had less than an hour ago. Vincent pulls him back, his hand barely brushing his shoulder.

I glance at Luc, but he looks away from me, his jaw tightening.

Matteo laughs, delighted. "Do I sense some dissension in your ranks? Your moral high ground appears to be sinking quickly, *cugina*."

"*You cold-hearted bitch.*" My heart stumbles over that, as Tony throws insults at me.

My heart pounds. I refuse to look in Luc's direction, to see the disgusted look he's currently giving me. The judgment.

Come on.

Come *on*.

I glance at Frankie. She's staring down at Tony now, a numb expression on her face.

She doesn't seem shocked. As if... as if she never expected to survive this anyway.

Rolling my eyes, I look back to Matteo. "You asked me to decide. I did. Your move."

His brow creases, as he searches for any hint of stress in my face. I don't give him any. "You're telling me that you are refusing to choose?"

"I'm telling you that I don't care either way." My voice is cool. "Perhaps the last few months have taught me something after all, Matteo."

He studies my face. Waves a hand. "Drop them."

Go – go—

A hard shove, as Amie and Frankie are thrown from the edge of the balcony—

Dante and Gio are ready. Their shots ring out, and my heart flies into my mouth as two men erupt into motion from our line as the guns go off. Rocco and Tony run straight for them.

I rip my knife back and throw it as hard as I can. Matteo stumbles back and out of sight, and Stefan bellows to the men behind us. "*Now!*"

The world turns to gunfire as our first line unloads their semi-automatic Glocks into the house. Bullets spray the stone walls, glass shattering and paint flying in every direction. Wave after wave keeps Matteo's men from returning fire, sheltering from the continuous assault and unable to get a shot in.

I stand motionless in the center of a hail of bullets as they pass by me, and a hard body tackles me to the ground.

Dom roars in my ear. "Keep your fucking head down!"

I don't. I twist in his grip, twist to try and see.

It was always a Hail Mary.

A single second. A million-to-one fucking chance.

A bullet fast enough to sever the unfurling rope from a distance that could be impossible.

And someone fast enough to catch them.

My head twists up, desperately trying to see through the smoke. The bullets still rage above our heads, angled away from the ground to stop Rocco and Tony being hit. "Did they get them?"

I don't see them. Can't see anything through the haze. Dom grabs my arm, pulling me back along the ground. "We're running out of ammo."

And as soon as we do, Matteo's men will return fire.

Voices ring out. Dante. Gio. Luc. Stefan. Dom returns their shouts, still pulling me along. "Fall back, first line!"

"Second!"

"Back!"

The smoke offers enough cover for us to scramble to our feet and run.

Please.

Please.

I burst free of the cloud at the edge of the house boundary, ducking through the gate and spinning around. I'm already scanning as the others emerge. Around us, soldiers run for the vehicles we left on the other side of the gate and jump in.

Gio and Dante appear first, panting. Gio shakes his head. "I don't know, Cat. I couldn't see."

There's agreement on Dante's face. And guilt, so much guilt. "It could have worked. But at that distance, the speed—,"

Luc appears next to them, Vincent beside him. The hope in my chest starts to fade. "Rocco? Tony?"

"They weren't behind us," Vincent says heavily. "We waited as long as we could."

Luc grips my face, the lie of his anger nowhere to be seen. Only grief fills his eyes. "We tried, Cat. You tried."

That's not good enough.

If I had chosen, I might have saved one. Instead, I chose to risk them both on the slim chance of getting them both out, and it didn't fucking *work*.

I tried to save two... and lost four.

"We have to go." Dom's voice isn't harsh. There's pain there, too. "They'll be coming this way any second."

"Not yet. We wait." My voice is iron. "Another minute."

"Cat—,"

"Another fucking *minute*," I snap. "Rocco and Tony might make it out, even if—."

If they were too late. If the shots didn't land.

"Tony wouldn't have left her there, Cat," Vincent says gently. "He's not coming back."

My eyes start to burn. Fuck. *Fuck.*

I can't think about it. Not now. "Rocco, then."

"One minute," Dante says hoarsely. He doesn't say it, doesn't mention Rocco at all, but he turns to face the rapidly clearing smoke, his fists clenched.

Thirty seconds tick past too quickly.

Sixty.

Ninety.

Slowly, I look at the men around me and swallow down the agony in my throat. "It's time."

"No." Dante doesn't move from his spot. His fists are clenched, his back straight. "Not yet."

I swallow, before turning to Dom. "We'll be there in a minute."

He scans my face, but he doesn't argue. He grips a silent Vincent's shoulder as I turn from them and walk over to where Dante stands.

He inhales as I slip my hand into his. "We spent our whole childhood together, Cat. I'm not leaving him. If he's not here, I'm going back."

"It's too late," I say, my throat aching. "He would have been here by now."

"I'm not leaving him in that place," he repeats hoarsely. "Get in the car."

I don't respond. Instead, I pull out my gun and check it's still loaded. I've lost a knife – and hopefully Matteo is bleeding out because of it – but I still have several on me. "We go now, then. Before they get a chance to regroup."

I'm hoping the fucker is dead, but I'm not holding out hope. We're not that lucky. But if he's injured, the ensuing chaos might be enough for the two of us to get through unnoticed.

"Absolutely fucking not." He stares at me. "Get in the damn car."

He swears when I walk past him, grabbing my arm. "I'm not joking."

"You're right," I tell him. "And if you think I'm letting you go alone, you would be wrong. Try and stop me and I'll shoot you."

I'm not losing anyone else today.

Our heads jerk up at the same time. A heavy sound comes from behind the trees on our left. Almost... dragging.

We move at the same time.

Frankie Costa hisses at us as we rip the branches back. "Help me!"

Unhurt.

I sag, almost stumbling. "I – what—,"

Dante throws Tony's arm over his shoulders, dragging him upright. Tony's face is ashen, sweat beading on his upper lip as he stretches his hand out for Frankie.

She takes it without looking at him. "I landed *on* him. His leg snapped."

"Worth it." Tony hisses as he tries to take a step. His leg is bent out of shape. "I'm fine. But Rocco needs help."

Dante nearly drops him. "Is he hurt?"

Tony shakes his head. "Amie's in bad shape."

I take off at that, ducking through the dense trees. Searching.

"Don't you fucking *dare*."

I hear him before I see him. Rocco looks up, his face strained. He doesn't stop, his hands locked onto Amie's chest as he pumps. Chest compressions. "Eye of the Tiger, right?"

He drops his mouth to hers, covering her nose and blowing air into her lungs until they rise. "Don't fucking die on me now, *bella*. Not after surviving that fucking fall."

"You caught her," I breathe. I take over the breathing as Rocco hums a familiar tune, his hands never losing rhythm. "Oh my god. It worked?"

"Damn luckiest shot I ever saw." Rocco stares down at her face. "Damn it, Amie. *Come on*."

I press my fingers against her ravaged neck, feeling the sluggish beat. "It's weak but it's there."

"It's enough." He lifts her easily before we make our way back, Rocco almost quicker than me despite her weight. Dom and Dante are arguing beside the car, both of their faces turning to shock as we burst from the trees.

I rip the car door open, my words aimed at Vincent in the front seat. "Take her straight to the hospital. I'll meet you there."

"I'll hold her." Dom offers, but Rocco grips her.

"No."

When they're inside, the car pulling off before I've even closed the door properly, I press my hands to my face.

"You did it." Dom's voice is thin with shock. "Cat. Dante, that shot- both of you. You and Gio – all of it. *Fuck*."

A Hail Mary.

One in a million.

We slide into the other car, Gio shifting over to make space as Dante gets in the front. "Where now?"

"The hospital." I meet Dom's eyes in the mirror. "And then we're making a call."

I'm ready for this to be done.

CATERINA

I pull the door closed behind me with a soft click. My eyes feel gritty, my head pounding.

"How is she?"

Turning, I glance over at Rocco. His clothes are stained with dirt as he sits with his hands propped on his knees. A lit cigarette dangles between his fingers.

In the fucking *hospital*. "You can't smoke here, you know."

"Shit." He stubs it out on the floor. "So?"

My shoulders tighten. "She'll live, so that's something. Thanks to you."

For what it's worth. She has months of recovery ahead of her. Physical. Mental.

She'll never be the same again.

Rocco shrugs. "I didn't do anything apart from sing that fucking song. Can't get it out of my head, now."

I glance up and down the empty hall. "I... yeah. Dom's waiting for me outside. Are you coming back with us?"

Shaking his head, he pulls out a lighter, flicking it on and off. "I'll stay for a while. Hey, Cat?"

I turn. "Yeah?"

He wiggles his eyebrows at me. "I've been looking after your friend for Gio, but he's not in great shape. Figured you should know. You know, in case you want to be the one to kill him."

My eyebrows draw down as I try to follow his sentence. "What? Who? *Why*?"

"How, where, when—,"

"*Rocco*—,"

"Relax." He grins, and there's something savage behind it that makes me wonder exactly what his story is. "You know, the whiny fucker. Can't remember his name. Used to be the Fusco enforcer."

I stare. "*Leo*?"

He points at me. "That's the one. I've been calling him *little carrot cock* for the last few weeks because I forgot it."

I grimace at the visual. "How do you – actually, never mind. Thanks."

"Welcome."

***

My stomach churns as Vincent pulls the door open, a surprised look on his face. "Hey."

"They here?" I glance past him. I've only been to the apartment shared by Vincent and Tony a handful of times over the last six years. It's surprisingly tidy, the sides clean and a basket of clean washing on the table.

Vincent follows my look. "Yeah. Uh...Danny was the messy one."

Neither of us mention Nicolo.

He points me in the direction of Tony's room. "Hey, Cat. How... how's Rosa doing?"

I pin him with a hard stare, and he glares back at me. "I just wanted to know if she's doing okay. That's *it*."

"She's fine," I say flatly. "And still sixteen."

"*Merda*," he mutters. "I know that."

"Remember it. Especially now you've seen how precisely Gio can shoot when he wants to."

Hiding my smile at his expression, I head past him and knock on the door.

Frankie pulls it open. "Oh, thank fuck. Maybe he'll listen to you. He's a stubborn *figlio di puttana*. There's no fucking *way* he can walk on that leg, but I think his ears are broken as well as his damn tibia—."

Her words cut off as I throw my arms around her. "It's good to see you, Frankie Costa."

Her arms lift, resting against my back.

She's smiling slightly, her scar stretching when I pull away. "You too, Corvo. Glad you got out."

Our eyes meet. "Only because of you. The nails helped. Thank you."

She glances down at her own, bare nails, her fingers curling over until they're hidden from view. "Then it was worth it."

There's more to say, and both of us know it. Perhaps both of us understand the other in a way none of the men around us possibly could, unless they experienced it themselves.

But today is not the day to rake up those thoughts. Instead, I join her in telling off an irritated Tony. He takes it with a scowl, but he doesn't move his eyes away from Frankie. "I can still fight."

"No," I say firmly. "You can't, Tony. You'd be a liability."

Frankie rolls her eyes. "*Grazie*. Common sense, Antonio."

I catch them both watching each other. "I'll come back tomorrow and check in."

After saying goodbye to Vincent, I call Gio. He answers on the first ring. "Where are you?"

"Walking past the Courtyard. Why has Rocco been looking after Leo?"

He pauses. "*Merda*. Is he dead?"

I frown. "Rocco didn't seem to think so. But he said something about him not... having long."

He blows out a breath. "I'll meet you in the Courtyard."

I only wait a few minutes before he appears at the edge. I feel his eyes on me as I walk in a slow circle around the oak tree.

The mannequins have been taken away, Sandro's body prepared for burial.

So many to call for.

Gio sighs. "I always liked this spot."

Our neutral place. "We've had some encounters here, Giovanni Fusco."

He narrows his eyes at me, but a smile plays on his lips. "Like when you told me you'd stolen all of the Fusco money."

"Or when you kidnapped me." I snort. "And then carried me back across the campus because you thought I was dying."

"I was so damn angry with you." He takes a step. Another, until he's looking down at me. "I think I knew then, you know."

I fold my arms. "Oh?"

"You were already taking up far too much space in my head, Corvo." Gio pushes some hair away from my face. "And then you gave me a heart attack by bargaining with Matteo, and I finally pulled my head out of my ass."

I look up at him, sliding my hands around his waist.

"I was a fool," he murmurs. "You were always going to be inevitable, Caterina Corvo."

Our lips brush. Once, twice, before I pull back. "I'm very curious about this Leo situation."

He raises his eyebrow at me. "He's a traitor."

"So you cut off his tongue?"

"Not yet." He takes my hand, heading off the path toward the trees. "I thought he was due some poetic justice first. And then I thought you deserved to have a say. So I've been... keeping him around."

"And Rocco?" I ask curiously. "I didn't know you were friends."

"Man's a psychopath," Gio mutters. "But... yes, I suppose. Acquaintances, anyway."

"Nothing like some male bonding over a little torture. How very traditionally Cosa Nostra of you."

He laughs. We step into a clearing I recognise, and I turn, my eyes landing on a barren piece of grass. I recognise it instantly, although many others now litter the ground around us. "This is where they buried me."

Where the world disappeared beneath a black hood, and Luc scarred his own hands to get me out.

"Yes." Gio walks over to a tree and picks up a shovel. "And now Leo knows exactly what it feels like. Quite a few times over, in fact."

My mouth opens as I consider the effort. "Seriously?"

He shrugs, but his eyes are dark. "He could have *killed* you. I had no idea – would have stopped it if I did. I'll do the same to any man who hurts you. Unless you kill them first, that is. And then he went to fucking *Matteo*. They deserved each other."

I wait as he shovels piles of dirt from a growing hole. "I think this is possibly both the sweetest and the strangest present I have ever received, you know."

His lip curls up in amusement, a streak of dirt across his cheek. "I'll try to keep the surprises going, but no promises."

"Too late," I murmur, "That bar is sky high now."

We both take a side of the coffin that emerges around the depleting dirt, heaving it out of the ground. It doesn't feel nearly as heavy as I expect it to. A foul odor wafts up, and my nose wrinkles. "Well, that's fucking disgusting. How long have you been doing this, exactly?"

Gio eyes the box. "Since the night you were taken. Maybe a week or two after. I was letting him out and then putting him back in, but Rocco doesn't strike me as the most organized. He might be dead."

"Only one way to find out."

Gio pushes the lid off, and we both look in.

"I think... he might be dead," I whisper.

I almost hope so. He doesn't look anything like the Leo who buried me that night. Shrunken and pale, his body covered in his own waste. But his eyelids flicker.

I smile grimly down as they blink open. "Hello, Leo."

Watery pupils fix on me. A muffled grunt comes from behind the grubby gag in his mouth. My eyes travel up to his forehead. Gio frowns, leaning in to look at the fading orange squiggles. "What the fuck is that?"

I clear my throat. "A drawing... of a little carrot cock. I think."

He stares at me incredulously, and I shrug. "Rocco."

We both turn our attention back to Leo.

"Your decision," Gio says.

I click my tongue as Leo's eyes dart between us. "We could just... leave him here. Poetic justice."

But as my eyes travel over him, I sigh. "No. I can't. He's too pathetic to live."

Leo starts to squirm, adding credence to my words. Begging noises drag from his throat. "You think he'd want to die, after all this."

"Rocco said the same thing."

Huh. Maybe I do have something in common with Dante's enforcer.

But it gives me an idea. I pull out my knife, the handle twirling between my fingers. "How's this, Leo? You can die right now, or you can die in that box and live another few hours. Your choice."

"I would end it now," Gio says to him quietly. "Because I won't be opening this box again."

His head jerks between us both. Considering.

"Nod for yes. Shake for no." I wave the knife for emphasis. "It'll be quick."

He stares at the blade, his breathing quickening.

And then... he shakes his head.

I sit back on my heels, staring at him in disgust. "*Seriously?*"

Gio shakes his head. "You're a fucking cockroach, Leo."

I point the end of my knife at him. "Remind me never to trust your people-reading skills, Fusco. *Ever.*"

On the final word, I slam the knife down without looking. It goes straight through the gag and into his neck.

The small amount of light left in his eyes fades quickly.

Gio's brows lower as I stand, brushing the dirt off my knees and sinking my blade into the ground to wipe off the Leo juices. "That was probably the kindest thing for him."

And yet, still extremely satisfying.

CATERINA

My apartment hasn't changed. My things are exactly where I left them. I run my fingers over the blue robe tossed over the chair.

Nothing is out of place. But I turn, my eyes narrowing. "Who's been staying here?"

"Me." Gio tilts his head in curiosity, and a hint of wariness. "How did you know?"

"Because it's far too *clean*, for one. I quite like my corner dust bunnies. Closest I get to having pets." I head into my bedroom. "I need to get ready for the meeting."

"Dom said he got hold of everyone." He follows me in.

I blow out a breath. "Some will join because they want to. Others will because they don't want to miss out. And others will report straight back to Matteo."

Hopefully.

"Assuming he's alive." Gio takes a seat on the bed, leaning his elbows on his knees.

"He is." My voice is grim. "My knife wasn't at the right angle to get his heart. Shoulder wound at best."

But he's injured, at least.

I disappear into the shower, sinking into the familiarity of my own things. My own shampoo. My own hairbrush.

When I walk out forty minutes later, I pause in my doorway. "Well. This is cozy."

Luc glances up. "Come and eat. We have time."

The others are seated around my table. And the familiar sight creates a suspicious prickle at the back of my throat, even though another seat has been filled.

I watch Stefan with a smile.

He fits here. All of them fit here. How strange that they once seemed so out of place.

That they ever felt like anything but mine.

Several cold beers are scattered across the table, and Luc nods to the chilled bottle of white in the middle. "Pour us both one?"

I press my lips to his shoulder as I glance over. He tosses the pasta, coating it. "Lucia taught you very well."

"She did." He piles the carbonara into a bowl. "This was a quick one, though."

"Have you spoken to her?"

He nods, his warmth soaking into me. "I did. Dante did, too, and Stefan. Do you want to call?"

My chest constricts. "No. Not if everything is fine."

He sets the pan down, turns to face me. "Little crow."

Smiling, I shake my head. "It's not that. I'll be distracted. Later, maybe. After the call."

He studies me. "Fair enough."

I slip into the seat beside Stefan. His arm immediately wraps around the back of my chair. "I like your apartment."

"Me too. You can blame Gio for the cleanliness, though."

The daylight fades as we eat, all of us quiet as we demolish the food.

It's been a long day. A long *year*. And depending on how the next few hours go, we might not get the chance to sit like this for a while.

Stefan toys with my hair. "Is there anything I can do? Before the call?"

"No." I frown. "If they don't listen, we're in trouble. I never thought I'd pray to have a snake in the Corvo ranks, either."

Someone to carry the message I'll be sending.

"If they don't listen, they are fools," he says shortly. "You'll persuade them, Cat."

He has a lot of faith in me. They all do.

Dante stops at the door as they're leaving. "We could stay."

"You know as well as I do that you can't." I sigh. "We need to be ready, Dante. Everyone needs to be ready."

He presses his lips to mine. "We'll do what is needed. Take your time."

I get changed as Dom is setting up, slipping on a fitted black silk blouse over sleek black trousers. After a moment, I add my black heels, too.

Something I can move in. Fight in.

My hair is slicked back into a bun, sharp pins keeping it in place and my make-up smoky. "Will I do?"

His eyes skate over me as he sets the laptop down. "Always, but yes."

I take a breath. In, and out.

I will have one chance at this. *One*.

One final game. There will be no more hiding for Matteo or I if this works as we intend it.

It will be the end. One way or another.

"Thirty seconds," Dom murmurs. I sit in front of the darkened screen and wait.

The screen flickers to life in front of me. My own face appears first. And then, slowly, others.

One by one, more faces. Faces I recognise from my childhood. Some of whom I have known all my life.

My uncle crosses his arms when he appears, smiling at me. "*Buonasera*, Caterina."

"*Buonasera*. It's good to see you, Marco."

We say nothing else, aware of the eyes on us. My face remains impassive as I sit silently.

Everyone. I can't see anyone missing. Every senior Corvo soldier, anyone with men under them, sits in front of me. Close to a hundred, spanning every part of the country. The majority are based locally in our territory, but we maintain a presence elsewhere.

Every member of the senior Corvo hierarchy looks back at me.

Finally, I incline my head. "*Benvenuto*, everyone. Thank you for joining me."

I take a moment to cast my eyes over the sea of faces. "I appreciate that this was last minute."

"Indeed." Eduardo Cavalli clears his throat. "I'm sure that I speak for us all when I say that we're interested to know why this meeting is taking place."

I take a breath. "I am asking for your help. All of you. And I would ask that you listen to me speak, before you make a decision."

Murmurs. Some nods. Some of the faces don't change. Others look unhappy. Some, curious.

Steepling my fingers, I begin. "You are aware that Matteo Corvo recently claimed the role of the *capo dei capi* and capo of the Corvo family. A role that he installed himself in after murdering my father and two other capos in cold blood at a peaceful meeting."

I pause, letting the information sink in before I continue.

"The Cosa Nostra is built on the bonds and rules we have created over hundreds of years. Alliances. *Family.* Matteo Corvo has ripped that apart in the name of power. He runs unchecked, spilling blood at every opportunity. Murdering children. There is a tenuous balance in our world, a balance we need. A balance between upholding tradition, respect for the hierarchy and adapting to the world as it changes around us."

"Family," I say quietly. "Honor. Loyalty."

"Matteo cares nothing for any of it. And none of us will remain untouched by his greed. He will come for your families if you do not follow him. Maybe not today, but one day. He will take your daughters, twist your sons into men that you do not wish to recognise. He will *destroy* the Cosa Nostra if left unchecked, and I will not stand by and watch our legacy burn."

"Pretty words," someone interrupts. I scan the screen. "Good evening, Ricardo."

The older man doesn't smile. "A lovely speech, Caterina, but a little redundant. You are no longer a Corvo, I understand, but an *Asante*. If the rumors are correct, you even wear their brand in your skin. And as such, this discussion should not include you, Caterina Asante."

Rustling sweeps across the screen. More nods.

"Ricardo." I tap my chin. "You have three daughters, correct?"

Taken aback, he stiffens. "I do. What of it?"

"Tell me," I say shortly. "If your daughters were taken, and forced into a marriage with falsified records, would you stand for it? If they were beaten, branded, drugged and *raped,* would you stand by and watch that happen?"

"I – of course not," he blusters. He looks at the other faces on the screen. "It would be cause for retaliation, as well you know. Wars have been started for less between the Families."

"Indeed." My tone is ice-cold. "And if they were carved up, the pieces of their body scattered across your gardens, would you accept that? Where does the line sit?"

Plenty of them shift uncomfortably at my stark words. Ricardo reddens.

"We are not talking about the Fusco—."

"*Any one of your children could be Nicoletta Fusco,*" I snap back at him. "Any one of them could be *me*. Amie Corvo, my father's widow, is lying in the hospital as we speak and may never *see* again because of what Matteo did to her. He tortured her for his own entertainment, and he will do worse if he is not stopped."

I force myself to take a breath. "As for my own circumstances – my so-called marriage, as you pointed out. Your daughters are lucky to have you, Ricardo. My father's body was still cooling when Salvatore Asante took me by force at Matteo's request. I had to retaliate for myself. You could always ask my *husband* how that worked out, if you can find the parts of him I left behind when I was finished."

Silence. I meet their assessing looks. "Does anyone have any other questions about my marriage? And be warned. There is a line between assurance and disrespect."

Ricardo flushes deeply, his words stuttering. "Ah – no."

"Good. I may wear the Asante brand in my skin now," I say quietly. "But my *name* is Caterina Corvo. I will always be a Corvo, until the day that I die. It is a promise I have lived by my entire life. Matteo sold me off in an attempt to prove otherwise, and yet I am *here*. I'm fighting for our future, for your future, while he burns the Corvo legacy to the ground."

Elio Maranzano is first to speak in the silence that settles over the call as I finish. "What exactly is your plan, if I may ask?"

"You may. Two nights from now, my men and I will be visiting Matteo. This uncertainty has gone on for too long, and every day, more blood is shed. I intend to put an end to it."

"With what allies?"

I lean back. "Dante V'Arezzo. Luciano Morelli. Giovanni Fusco. And Stefano Asante, the *new* capo. I'm happy to assure you that he bears no resemblance to his predecessor. They have agreed to the use of their men. Matteo has a significant number of paid men in his pocket which we need to counter, as well as several Corvo men."

My eyes narrow. "Some of them, I can see on this call."

More sit up at that. Several drop off the call altogether.

"There is a new alliance in place." I tap my finger on the table. "Across the Cosa Nostra. A *permanent* alliance, to help us weather the challenges we face on the outside. Opportunity. Growth. Strength. We have spent too long on petty squabbles and disagreements, and it has caused a chasm across our world that others like Matteo have exploited."

I wait for the murmurs to die down. "Assuming, of course, that I remain the Corvo capo. Should Matteo continue, I can assure you that our world will look quite different in the very near future."

I gaze into the screen. "I will not beg for your support. But we will fight in two nights, and I will remember who stood by and waited for the coin to land before choosing a side. I expect an answer this evening."

I've barely ended the call before my phone rings. "Marco?"

"Well done." My uncle doesn't waste time. "That was quite the speech, Caterina. Some will be angry at the deception, but if he takes the bait, it won't matter."

"I hope so." I meet Dom's gaze. His gray eyes glitter as he straps on his weapons. "We'll find out, but we need to move fast for this to work, Marco. How quickly can you get your men here?"

"We're leaving right now. I was holding off for the call. I'm already receiving messages from some of the others."

"I trust your judgment on who to tell. But we need to tread carefully."

We would fight in two nights, I told the Corvo soldiers.

A warning to Matteo. To draw him out, to get him here. Expecting us to be unprepared. He'll walk straight in and finish this like a coward, crowing over his underhanded plan as his hired thugs finish us before our allies can get here.

Finish *me*.

Our victory, or our failure. Everything hinges on Matteo's next move. If he comes tomorrow, we'll be waiting with an army to match his own.

If he comes tonight... we'll be alone, until the rest can get here. And my gamble could cost us everything.

"Move fast, Marco," I breathe.

"I'll be there in three hours."

Stefano

"Thanks for coming with me."

Luciano Morelli glances over at me from the passenger seat. "I can go in, if it's easier."

I don't tell him how much I appreciate the offer. "No. It's just a building."

The fake agents planted by Matteo have left, tatters of tape the only sign that they were here at all as we drive up to the compound. It desecrates the landscape around it, monstrous gray walls towering up into the night sky.

My home. Or it used to be.

Now, my home is wherever she is.

I don't feel the same sense of foreboding I once did as we pull up to the gates, broken and twisted. Alongside us, chunks of wall still litter the ground from the explosions that blasted holes in the compound walls.

Several other cars pull up behind, ready to load whatever we can carry. "You think it'll be tonight?"

Luc looks over at me as we get out. "Maybe. He might wait until tomorrow, give himself more time to prepare but still get here before the Corvo men do. Or if he panics, he might move now. I know what I'd put my money on."

I feel the same way as I nod toward the doors, hanging from their hinges. "Then we'd better hurry."

Luc whistles as I lead him down to the storage areas through the corridors. Sections have been blown apart completely, dark stains on the floor highlighting the clean-up operation afterward. "Fuck me. This place really is like a military compound."

"That was the idea." I pull open the door, and we both stare at the supplies inside.

Hundreds of crates sit in front of us.

Guns. Explosives. Tasers. Anything and everything that we might need. Might already need, depending on how quickly Matteo moves - if he even takes the bait at all.

My throat tightens, the urge to get back to Cat as soon as possible gnawing at my stomach. "Let's move."

~~G~~iovanni

"Lorena." I fight the urge to pinch my nose. "It's not going to be safe. You have to leave."

She pushes past me, smacking my ankle on the way past with her stick. "At the speed I walk, they'll catch up to me at the gates. No, I'm staying right here."

Her eyes gleam as she turns back to me. "You tell that Corvo girl to make sure he doesn't get back up. Weasel little cunts like him always do."

I cross my arms. "I can get someone to drive you out."

She coughs. "And go where? They're not going to storm an old woman's apartment, Fusco. They'll have bigger fish to fry. And so do you. So get gone and leave me the hell alone, unless you bring coffee with you."

She uses her cane to slam the door in my face.

Fucking hell.

Cat walks up as I'm about to enter the main hall, her expression tense. Around us, men head up and down the steps, following whatever instructions they've been given.

She sighs. "It's done. Now to see if he takes us up on our offer."

A waiting game.

"How did they respond?"

"Hard to tell." Her eyes scan the bustling activity. "I suppose we'll find out. Marco seemed positive. He's on his way."

Tables have been shoved to the walls, weapons and supplies set up on every available surface. In the corner, a group of my junior soldiers are stacking dry food and bottled water.

Cat notices them too. "How long can we hold out if we need to?"

"Long enough. There's plenty there." And not that many of us. But I don't need to say it.

"How many do we have?" Cat looks around, and I lead her over to where Dom is leaning over a blueprint spread out across the table. "Maybe fifty here who can fight. We've called in the men we took to the Asante compound, anyone who was close enough to get here, but we lost a lot. Others left. Overall, we're looking at around two hundred in total, if they get here in time. The rest are too far away."

Two hundred. Without the Corvo men, we're going to struggle. This is their territory.

"And we think Matteo has at least four hundred." Dom's face is grim. "That's the number he talked about when I was there. We'll hold them off as long as we can."

Four hundred against half of that. "We're not without our own tricks. Nico and Johnno are preparing the entrance for when they arrive."

Cat rubs at her neck. "Let's pray it's tomorrow, and the Corvos decide that they'd prefer me to Matteo."

I brush her cheek. "They will. We'll be ready, Cat. If he comes tomorrow night, then it will work perfectly. And if he comes tonight, we can hold on."

"I hope so."

Domenico

Vincent jogs up to me. "Everyone who needed to be gone has left from our side. Tony wasn't happy, but Frankie talked him around."

We stand for a moment, watching the junior soldiers load up their guns. "They all look fucking petrified."

"As they should." Vincent keeps his voice low. "Cockiness gets you killed, Dom. Fear will keep them alive and fast."

I glance at him, incredulous. "Is that the bullshit you taught them?"

He huffs a laugh. "Yeah. Think it'll work?"

I hope so. I watch as one fumbles, dropping his gun. Paul Maranzano puts down his own weapon, stalking over and grabbing it from the floor. He checks to see if it's loaded before rapidly slipping a load in, stacking it and handing it back to the soldier.

Vincent hums thoughtfully. "We need to recruit, when this is over."

A new face in Danny's seat.

If there's anyone left to recruit.

And if we're left to recruit them.

I turn back to the blueprints. With not enough men, I focus on the strategic areas. Cat leans in beside me, pointing. "Put a group there. They can fence them in."

Nodding, I make a nod, before calling over one of the few seniors we have left. Cat watches in silence as he walks off.

I pull her into me and wrap my arms around her, uncaring of the eyes that pause to look over. "We're as ready as we're going to be."

She leans her head against my chest. "Stefan and Luc aren't back yet."

"They're on their way. I had a message from Luc. They've got plenty."

Weapons we need to push back Matteo's men. "If Marco's men get here after it starts, it might not be the worst thing. They can sweep in from the back."

Too many possibilities. But whatever happens, I find that I'm more than ready to end this. "If I get a chance to take him out, I'm taking it."

She nods against my chest. "He'll come straight for me, you know."

I know. "That's why I'm not leaving your side."

Dante

"You should sleep, *tentazione*."

I settle down next to Cat on the steps. She keeps her arms wrapped around her legs, the night air cool enough that goose pimples rise up on her skin. "I'm waiting for Stefan and Luc."

I scan the space in front of us. The campus is dark and silent, all activity focused on the hall behind us. Everyone has their positions, ready to move as soon as we need to.

"Dom has a camera on the gates. We can wake you."

"I don't think I can sleep anyway," she says quietly. "There are too many thoughts in my head."

I nudge her. "Share them. Make some space."

A tired smile tugs at her lips. "What if we've misjudged this? He might not come at all."

"Then we get to take an army to him," I point out. "Seems like an excellent option to me."

She sighs. "I just want him dead. I want to be free of him. I want a *life*, Dante."

Cat leans into me as I wrap my arm around her shoulders. "He's not walking out of this, *tentazione*. Another day or two at most, and we're free. We'll go and get Alessia, and we'll bring her home."

She smiles. "Here?"

"Why not? Temporarily, of course." I breathe her in, the familiar scent enough to calm the thumping of my heart. "We can take our time looking for a place for all of us."

A home for the future. One day soon, we'll walk out of these gates for the last time.

Leaving a place full of memories, to create new ones.

"That sounds nice," she murmurs. "And we can hold Cosa Nostra meetings over dinner. With wine. Luc can cook. Although we should probably take it in turns."

My lips twitch up. "Much more preferable to the old way of meetings."

She laughs. "I want a gavel. One of those things you bang on the table to call everyone to order. Makes it more official."

I can almost see it in my head. A future unburdened by the hell of Matteo Corvo. A future that the six of us can build. Solid foundations. A safe life for our daughter.

It sounds perfect.

Luciano

They appear in the distance behind us; a long line of bright white lights that flicker in the mirror next to my window as I lean forward, before twisting in my seat to look behind.

It's the middle of the fucking night. There's only one reason a row of lights would be heading our way.

"Stefan." My voice is tight. "How long until we get back?"

He glances in the rearview mirror, his voice tight. "Fifteen minutes."

Fuck.

He presses down on the accelerator, the car speed increasing until we're flying down the road. The others behind us in the convoy do the same as I yank out my phone.

Dom answers on the first ring. "Luc."

"They're coming. We're fifteen minutes out, and they're coming up behind us."

Dom hangs up.

I don't say anything as the speed of the car creeps up further. "We're going to make it."

"Maybe," he says grimly. "But they're going to be right fucking behind us."

CATERINA

We watch the camera footage in tense silence.

Lights appear on the road, the cars flying up way too fast. They won't be able to stop in time. My heart thumps. "Get those gates open."

"Open the gates." Dom shouts the order down the radio. "Now!"

Luc and Stefan barely clear them, the car doors scraping against the metal.

No sooner is the convoy through than they're being pushed shut again. Nico and Johnno, blurry small figures on the screen in front of us, fly into action, wrapping the metal as quickly as possible. Several others begin loading up the road, tossing packages down seemingly at random.

Behind me, Vincent is organizing, sending groups to go and help with the unloading of the convoy. Other groups leave to take up their positions around the campus.

I check my weapons again on my way out to help. Guns are strapped to my arms, my legs, spare cartridges at my waist along with anything

I thought might be useful. My daggers are in position, waiting at my heels.

"They're coming." Dom's voice makes me jerk back around. Dante and Gio crowd in behind me as we watch, the hall behind us falling silent.

The row of vehicles seems to go on forever. They don't *stop*.

Nico and Johnno are still working on the gates.

"Get out of there," Gio mutters. "Come on."

The small figures behind are still working. Still dropping those packages.

"Less than a minute." Dom's voice is strained. "How are we doing on the convoy?"

I turn to look. Boxes are coming into the hall, a group ripping them open to distribute as others hand them in. "It's unloading."

"Thirty seconds."

The figures on the screen scatter, disappearing into the darkness.

"Ten."

My breath catches in my chest as I count down.

"Here we go," Gio murmurs.

Three.

Two.

One.

The screen flashes white as the iron gates explode, the noise of the explosion hitting us a second later. I plant my feet into the ground as the room shakes, boxes spilling open on the table opposite.

Several other booms follow, as Matteo's men drive straight over the mines thrown down to welcome them.

"Let's hope he was in the front," Dante mutters.

He won't be. But as the screen wavers back into place, pieces of broken, smoking wreckage block the entrance. "How many did we hit?"

"Hard to tell." Dom studies it. "But enough to buy us some time. They can't drive through."

Any remaining soldiers are leaving, directed to locations across campus by Vincent and Gio. Only a handful remain. Vincent strides out with a nod to me. "See you on the other side, boss."

No goodbyes.

My fingers clench around my phone as I check my messages. "An hour, Marco says."

An hour until any reinforcements get here.

We're the only group left. "We need to get over there."

Stefano and Luc push through the doors with boxes in their hands, their eyes immediately moving to me.

"Fucking hell, that was close," Luc breathes when I head to them. "Stefano drives like a machine."

Stefan is already digging through boxes. He tosses me some Glock switches and I start attaching them to one of my guns, keeping the other for single use.

"Time to go." Dante grabs another of the switches. "They're coming in fast."

I glance over to the screen, to the dozens of crawling ants climbing over the smoking remains of the cars. Dom is watching them, his brows drawn down. "Dom. Let's go."

We won't be separated. Not this time.

Gio assesses some of the weapons in the box Stefan still holds, pulling out a couple. "Everyone got what they need?"

Nods. I stare around at them all, at their faces.

They all look back at me.

No goodbyes.

We take off from the hall at a run until we reach the Courtyard. The light is dim, but my feet move easily over the familiar ground as we spread out across the space.

Dante pulls me to a stop. "The path over there. Anything goes wrong, you're going to *run*."

My chest thumps. "Absolutely fucking not—,"

"*Yes*," he snaps. "You are, Cat."

They all stare at me steadily.

"You picked this on purpose." Dawning horror fills me. "You know I won't do that."

"I promised you would make it *back*." Dante grips my face. "If you need to, Cat, if it looks bad – that's your way back to her."

"Fuck you. You take the damn path."

He studies me. And then his lips smash into mine, brief and hard. "Stubborn, infuriating—,"

"Incoming," Stefan says urgently. We quieten, taking our places.

It feels organized. As if we can pick them off, one by one.

It begins that way. One appears, shot down in a moment by Dante. I take the next, my bullet ripping through his skull as he collapses.

Another, Stefan's shot landing in his chest.

And then they begin to pour into the Courtyard, a black wave of ants that crawl over us like the ants they felt like on the cameras. Black-clad men appear from every direction. Stefan and I put the semi-automatics to use as Dante and Gio pick off those closest. Dom and Luc focus on the sides of the large group that tries to flank us, keeping them close for our bullets.

Organized... until it isn't.

The minutes tick by, screaming filling my ears and smoke from the guns burning my eyes. The space around us fills as more spill in, both from our side and Matteo's.

Our guns are slowly replaced by hand-to-hand fighting in the tight quarters. I rip my knives out from a man who gets too close, turning to sweep my blade across the neck of another who grabs for me.

Dante and Luc are a few feet away, barely visible. I can't see Stefan at all. Gio and Dom stay close, our backs together for protection.

Boom.

Another explosion erupts. Red and orange flash across my vision as my feet leave the ground, the air ripped viciously from my lungs. I hit the floor with a roll, my skin scraping until I come to a stop under the oak tree, my ears ringing.

"*Cat.*" Dom bellows my name frantically. "Cat!"

"Here." I cough, pushing myself upright. "I'm here!"

My voice croaks, and then another two of this endless river of *fucking* soldiers appear, both aiming for me as I lift my gun in return.

It goes on, and on. My hair sticks wetly to my face, the scent of iron in my nose and my skin stinging from my roll across the ground. I don't stop – can't stop.

I can't see them. Any of them, although I can hear them, return their shouts with my own even as the oncoming wave stops them getting to me.

They're still here, still fighting.

So am I.

We're holding on. Holding them back, the minutes ticking away and pushing us closer to help.

But I'm starting to get tired, the constant smash of men against my blades creating a growing ache around my shoulders, my arms.

I back up as another soldier drops with a choked cry, ducking beneath the tree and dropping my hands to my knees. There's a small space here, enough for me to take a second as I suck the air into my lungs.

Movement in the corner of my left eye—

The blow hits from nowhere. It smashes into my side, knocking the wind out of me as I crumple, losing my gun in the process. I throw my hands out blindly, searching as I rip my second from the holster.

Another hit. This time across my face, whipping it to the side.

Blood.

Iron in my mouth, as a rough laugh rings out above my head.

I hear shouts. They're pushing for me, roaring my name across the clearing, but Matteo's group cuts between us, a never-ending line.

It's just me and him, beneath the red oak tree.

Spitting out the blood collecting in my mouth, I roll away and pull myself upright. "Took you long enough."

My side is *screaming*. His punch broke a rib, at least, and as he holds up his hand, I realize why.

The knuckleduster looks like solid silver, matching the sharper caps that flash as Matteo smirks at me. "Hello, *cugina*."

"Right on... time." My lungs scream for air as I run my eyes over him, searching for weapons. "Glad to see you got my message."

His eyes darken. "Such a pretty, inspiring speech you gave this evening. I'll be watching carefully to see who bothers to answer your little plea."

My grin is more like a baring of teeth. "You're not going to be alive to see it."

He rotates his shoulder. "Planning on poking me with your toothpick again?"

I glance behind me, searching.

"Oh, they're not coming," his smile is sly. "I made sure to bring plenty of extra men to keep my fellow capos busy."

He takes a step forward. "Just you and me, Caterina."

"Excellent." My hand slides down to my belt as I try to distract him. "Did you enjoy our party trick yesterday? Must have hurt, having your show ruined. Embarrassing, really."

He shrugs, moving closer to me. Leisurely, as though he has all the time in the world as the campus burns around us.

"Plenty more of those in the future, I assure you. I've got all sorts of plans, Caterina. Everyone who you care about. All of them. I'm going to hunt them down when you're dead, and I'm going to make them *scream*."

Leaning in, he grins manically. "And those men you spread your legs for – they're first on the list. They're going to last for months. As long as I can keep them alive. They'll beg to die, and I'm going to enjoy every moment of their pain. Maybe I'll keep your body around to really torment them."

"You're a fucking psychopath." Rage coats my vision as we face each other. I tug on the string around my wrist before pulling the knife free. "And you will take no more of mine."

I throw the knife. It flies past his shoulder, and he throws his head back on a laugh. "Fucking pathetic."

So amused that he doesn't bother to *look*.

"Not that. *This*."

I whip the thin length of silver in my hand out with every bit of strength I have. It slashes across Matteo's face in a clean, deep cut that carves into his face as he folds over with a roar.

I run for him, flinging myself onto his back and gripping his neck as I wrap the garotte around it and pull as hard as I fucking can.

Matteo chokes beneath my grip as the silver cuts into his skin – deeper.

His fist slams *up* and into my cheekbone, leaving fire in its wake before I dodge the second hit and slide off, backing up.

His hands grapple with the garotte, but it's too tight for his fingers to create a gap as it cuts off his air, scarlet appearing in a thickening line beneath.

He shoves the knuckleduster off his hand in his desperation to pull it off, and I lean down to pick it up, sliding it on and weighing it. "This is heavier than I expected. Not my favorite, but since you don't like my *knives—*,"

It smashes into his nose and Matteo *howls*, a choked, enraged cry. He doubles over as he staggers away and I stalk toward him.

I slide my dagger from my shoe. "I was going to take a long time over this, but I'd rather you were dead."

I slash my knife across his face. "For Amie."

Again, my heart filled with rage. "For Bea and Pepe."

Again. "For Frankie."

His screams turn high and reedy as my knife cuts away. There are too many, too many dead and hurt by his hand.

Alessandro. Danny. Paul Morelli. Frank V'Arezzo.

Joseph Corvo.

Matteo slumps to his knees, his fingers clawing at his face and neck. Blood coats him; his eyes, his face as I lean forward and seize his chin in my hand.

"Gio should be here for this," I grit out, keeping him still. "But since he's not...,"

He struggles as I shove my hand into his mouth and yank out his tongue. "This is for Nicoletta Fusco, you evil cunt. *Va all' inferno*, Matteo."

His screams turn muffled as my knife slices through his flesh. I shove his head back as his body collapses, gurgling sounds the only noise he makes.

Tossing his tongue to the side in disgust, I sit. I pull up my knees and lean against the trunk of the oak tree as I watch my cousin writhing in agony and drowning in his own blood.

I do not look away as the life drains from his eyes, as he twitches and groans. "I hope it fucking hurts, *stronzo*."

It is not a slow death, nor an easy one, and I drink in every moment of it.

His movements slow, second by second.

Until finally, they stop completely.

Reaching for my gun, I unload a bullet into him. A few more.

Just in case.

My head thumps back against the trunk.

"Burn in hell," I whisper. "Tell Salvatore I said hello."

Dante

I can't see.

Can't see anything in this crowd, the mass of men focusing on us - on the five of us - with an intensity that makes my neck crawl.

"*Gio.*"

I roar his name. He's several feet away from me, grappling with a man as his gun whips across his face.

He's out of ammo.

And he's not paying attention. Doesn't see the soldier aiming for him, the pistol trained on his back.

I lift my gun, but all I get is a click. The chamber is empty, all of us running low against the flood of men that just keep fucking *coming*.

I run, shoving between a fighting group, my chest thumping.

A gunshot.

No—

The shot misses his exposed back by a fucking *inch*, the soldier aiming again before I crash into his side. My fist punches into his face, once, twice, blood spraying as we wrestle before I rip the gun from his hand and shove it against his cheek, pulling the trigger.

He slumps beneath me as I roll over, my chest heaving.

A hand reaches out. "That was close."

I glower at him as Gio pulls me up. "Watch your fucking back, you idiot."

But relief fills me as he grins, his face covered with blood from the dozens he has cut through. "Where's Cat?"

Turning, I look. My chest begins to pound. "I don't know."

I can hear Stefan, hear him bellowing her name. Luc, too.

Dom is a few feet away, and I lift the pistol in my hand, taking out the soldier opposite him.

It's clearing. The solid mass is thinning, creating gaps around us as Dom heads our way. He's in worse shape, a scarlet stain spreading across his shoulder. "A bullet nicked me. Where is she?"

Where is she—

Shouts come from the other side of the Courtyard. "More."

"Fucking hell," Gio hisses. "They're everywhere."

Between us, we assess our weapons. Not much is left.

"We spread out and find her." Dom looks grim as he glances around. We're pinned on the far side from where we started, pushed back by piles of men who now litter the floor around us.

"Domenico! Gio!"

All of us turn, as Dom frowns. It clears, relief replacing it. "Marco!"

Caterina's uncle pushes his way through the widening gap. He's bloody but grinning as he nods at us. "The campus is nearly clear. Sorry we're late. I was – well. They all came. Or most, anyway. Hundreds of them. They came for her. For the capo."

They came for the capo.

The Corvos responded.

But she's not here. I move away from them as more of Marco's men flood the Courtyard. Pockets of fighting are still taking place, but more clears as I stride through.

Searching.

Where are you, *tentazione*?

I stride past the oak tree, nearly missing it in the darkness. "Dante!"

She's on her feet as I spin, and her face is swollen and cut, but she dives for me anyway as I grip her. There's panic in her face, her voice, but she's *here*.

Unharmed.

"Are they—,"

"They're fine." I run my hand over her hair, falling and loose from her bun. "We're all fine."

"He's dead," she breathes. "He's dead, Dante."

I stare over her shoulder, taking in the slumped body.

Matteo Corvo, finally dead.

"You did it." My hold tightens as I turn back to her. "Your uncle is here too. They came, Cat. They all came for *you*."

I push sticky, bloody strands of hair from her face, frowning over the nasty swelling of her cheek. She grins at me, bright and brilliant. "So let's clear the rest of them out. It's over, Dante."

It's over.

Exhaling, I pull her to me one more time. Breathing her in. She stiffens. "Careful. I think he broke a rib. Maybe two."

My mouth opens as someone shoves into my back, and I stumble into her.

I pull myself upright, cupping her cheek. "*Merda*. Sorry. You okay?"

But it doesn't come out properly. I shake my head, trying again.

Buzzing. My lips... they feel *numb*.

But it can't be me, because Caterina's voice sounds like it too as she says my name.

She says it over and over again.

Caterina

His mouth opens, those green eyes blinking as he looks at me. "Cat."

I try to take his weight as he collapses against me, his knees folding like the strings of a puppet.

No.

I lower him to the ground, my hands running frantically over his body. "Dante – no. *No.*"

Blood. There's so much blood, everywhere, all over my hands, and I can't work out where it's coming from and why there's so fucking much of it—

Warm hands grip mine, slippery with his blood. "*Tentazione.*"

But it's not right. It's slow, and slurred.

He doesn't say it *right*.

He says it like he's saying goodbye.

"*No.*" I scream it at him. "Don't you fucking dare. *Don't you dare.*"

Don't say it. Not like that. Never like that.

I'm sobbing as I push him onto his side and see the scarlet spreading across his white shirt. So much that I can't tell where it's coming from. "*Help me!*"

And he's looking at me, and I'm gripping his face, yelling at him to stop *fucking around* and stand up.

I've messed up his face. There's blood on his lips as he coughs.

I try to wipe it away, but more of it appears.

His fingers brush mine, and they feel so cold. "It's okay."

No.

It's not okay.

It will never be okay.

I fight as hands pull me away, kicking and screaming until let go and I drop down next to him, shaking him.

This is not how it ends.

This is not how we end.

And I scream. I scream over and over as my heart rips and shatters, as my soul cracks, because Dante V'Arezzo is *not allowed to leave me.*

This is not the lifetime you promised me.

We were to have a lifetime, he and I. All of us together, with the family we chose, with the daughter we fought for.

"Wake up," I scream at him. "Wake *up*."

But his eyes close.

And he doesn't move any more.

Stefano

*S**creaming.*

I've never moved so fast. All of us, pushing through to get to her, to them.

Please, God—

But it's not her. The relief that chokes my lungs turns to a pounding, numbing beat in my chest as I stop, the others next to me.

She kneels over him, shaking him. And the screaming turns to his name, over and over again.

Dante.

And the blood.

Over her. Over him. Both of them covered. "Get up. *Get up.*"

But Dante is still. Silent.

There is nothing to suggest that he hears her at all. No movement, no motion in his chest.

Gio and Luc move first, dropping down beside him.

"Cat." Dom's face is white as he steps forward and wraps his arms around her. She throws herself back, bucking against him. "*He's not dead – he's not—,*"

She screams until her vocal chords shred beneath the weight of it, until my ears fill with her agony. Raw, hoarse, screaming sobs.

"Let them work." I grab her face, shaking it. "They're working on him, Cat."

She's beyond listening. Dom stares at me desperately, his eyes glittering.

It was not supposed to be like this.

Gio kneels in the pool of blood, Luc ripping off Dante's shirt as they turn him, exposing the mass of broken flesh in his upper back.

Luc swears quietly. "Come on, *fratello*. You're not going out like this."

He wraps the torn shirt up, pressing it against the wound. Pressing down, until he's kneeling on it. "There's nothing else I can do. We can't fix this here. Get a car as close as we can. *Now*. And something to carry him."

Cat shoves out of Dom's grip, her breathing ragged. "He's alive?"

Luc looks up at her; raw, anguished truth on his face. "Cat...,"

He cannot promise her that.

I go for the car, sliding behind the wheel as Gio and Luc carry him with Dom holding onto Cat as her heart breaks apart in front of us.

"As quickly as you can, Stefan," Luc says quietly before she gets in. "He's not going to survive the journey."

"He will," I say grimly.

For the first time since I was a child... I pray.

CATERINA

D ante V'Arezzo is dead.

And if I could undo the last hour of my life, I would give *everything* I possess to bring him back.

Dom sits on the floor beside me, his head resting against the wall.

I stare straight ahead. At the room where they turn off the lights, one by one. Pulling the masks off their faces, their surgical gowns.

Dom's phone rings, and I half-listen as he murmurs to Stefan. "It's clear?"

An affirmative sound catches my ears. A question.

Dom's voice is heavy. "We're staying for a while."

After, we sit in silence.

My throat is raw. "How many?"

How many did we lose?

"Thirty-two," he says quietly.

"Any…," I can't say it.

He hesitates. "Nico. He wouldn't leave the gates until everyone else was clear. Got caught in the explosion on the road."

I close my eyes. Nico, Luc's enforcer.

"And...,"

Silence. "Paul Maranzano."

I close my eyes. "What happened?"

"He... he pushed one of the others out of the way. Took the bullet through his neck."

I don't say anything for a long time. "He would have been a good senior."

"Yeah." Dom's voice is rough. "He would have."

Hours pass. My cheek throbs, my ribs burning, but I refuse to leave.

I don't look up when someone settles on my other side.

Luc doesn't say anything either. He picks up my hand, holding it. And I squeeze, thinking of Nico, outside those gates.

Gio settles against the wall opposite me. Stefan sits beside him.

And they stay with me.

All of us, waiting.

When the door behind us shifts, I straighten. The doctor is older. Gray-haired, stern-looking with tortoiseshell glasses that he pushes up his nose as he glances down at us. "Dante V'Arezzo's next of kin?"

"All of us." Gio pushes to his feet. "We're his family."

I stare at the doctor, waiting, as Luc grips my fingers tightly.

It feels as if I'm falling, as he begins to speak. As if my world drops out from beneath me, all over again. Words like *coma* and *spinal damage* and *paralysis*.

"When can I see him?"

***

He doesn't belong here in this cold, sterile room. Those tubes don't belong in his mouth, his nose, forcing his lungs to inflate.

I don't need the monitor on the wall to tell me how strong his heart is, when I *know*.

I know exactly how strong Dante V'Arezzo's heart is.

Stefan's heat brushes my back. "He'll come through this. Whatever he needs – it doesn't matter."

Murmured agreement around me.

No, it doesn't matter. None of it matters.

As long as he *lives*.

Six months later

R eaching for the gavel, I bang it on the table as I clear my throat. "I hereby call this session of the Cosa Nostra to order."

Alessia claps her hands in my lap, reaching for the gavel eagerly. "Mine!"

Her new favorite word. I distract her with a cracker instead.

Gio lounges in his seat, taking a sip from his beer. "Do we have to do this *every* time?"

I point at him before I pick up my wine. "Be honest. You much prefer these meetings to the old ones."

Because we get to have them at home in my apartment, with alcohol. And I get to sit there in nothing more than Luc's shirt as he stands at the counter and makes us food.

He glances over his bare shoulder with a smile. I let my eyes skate over his olive skin, taking my time as I breathe in.

Some nightmares do fade.

Others take longer.

I lean forward to snatch a few olives, tossing one into my mouth. Gio's eyes linger on my bare skin as Luc's shirt falls off my shoulder before giving me a slow, heated smile. "Perhaps they're not so bad."

I toss an olive at his head, grinning when it bounces off. "Not in front of Alessia."

Later.

She cackles in my lap. "GeeGee."

Gio spins to Luc, his expression suspicious. "Did you teach her that?"

Luc's shoulders shake. "No comment."

I settle back in my seat. Alessia climbs up and plants a sticky kiss on my cheek, smacking her lips. "Mama."

My smile fills my whole face as I pretend to take a bite of her cracker. "Thank you."

This is our ritual. Every month.

New traditions, for a new era.

An alliance unlike any the Cosa Nostra has ever seen.

"Bear!"

My daughter squeals directly into my ear.

"Up?" Alessia holds her arms out to Stefan as he leans in to kiss my head. He hoists her up on his way to the refrigerator, both of them poking their heads in and Alessia emerging triumphantly with a juice box as he sets her down. She goes straight to Dom to show him.

"I'm going to miss it here." I lean back with a sigh, looking around my apartment. So many memories.

But all good things must come to an end. And space is definitely an issue.

"You *like* the new house," Dom reminds me. "You chose it. You went to see it."

"Four times," Gio murmurs, as the door opens.

"It's going to be a base for all of us," I defend myself. "It needs to be right."

Lips press against my neck, and I lean back, closing my eyes, as he settles next to me.

Dante snags Alessia around the waist as she tries to run past him. She belly laughs as he blows a raspberry against her stomach. "Dada!"

His eyes soften as he looks over and catches me watching them. "Stop that. I'm fine."

"Good. Three months of hospital food was enough for a lifetime." I blink away the mist. "I seem to have dust in my eyes. Gio, the dust bunnies need to be groomed."

He glowers at me. "I'm buying you a vacuum for the new house."

"Try it. Don't complain when you wake up with it attached to your—." I stumble as a pair of wildly inquisitive green eyes fix on me. "*Little finger.*"

Laughter, as Gio throws an olive back at me.

Dante leans over, letting Alessia climb from his lap to mine as he captures my lips. "*La vita è bella, tentazione.*"

Life *is* good.

All of us, still here. Slowly building a new future, just the way we want.

A new generation of the Cosa Nostra, with five *equal* votes.

Alessia eventually falls asleep in Dom's lap. I push my chair back as he stands, following him into the bedroom and through the door to what used to be my closet, leaning against the frame as he settles her into the crib. "You okay?"

He studies me as I back out, following before his hands settle on my hips. "Why do you ask?"

I shrug. "I don't know. These meetings. I never want you to feel...,"
Like you don't have a voice.

He looks amused. "You offered. I said no. Besides, I still say what I think."

Five families.

Five capos.

"Do you feel like I'm less?" he asks quietly. "Would you have preferred I said yes, even though I don't want it?"

"No," I say immediately. "Of course not."

"Good." He swoops in, his lips pressing to mine as his tongue slips between my lips. His hands reach up, holding my face carefully. "Because I am exactly where I want to be, Caterina Corvo. I don't care about the rest of it."

Jesus. These men and their words. He nudges me back, and my thighs bump against the edge of my bed. My nose wrinkles. "More space. Definitely more space."

We improvised, the bed nearly swallowing up the whole room. With the others in and out, traveling between their bases and here... we've made it work.

"The new bed is bigger." Dom smirks. "I checked."

"Oh?" Slowly, I widen my legs in a silent invitation as he presses between them. The thin underwear underneath this shirt suddenly feels like no barrier at all, the heat of him through his gray sweatpants already swollen as it nudges against me.

My back hits the bed in a rush of air, my lips pursing as Dom follows me down. My bare foot slams out against his chest. "Still in your caveman era, I see."

He bats it out of the way easily, his hands finding my wrists as he presses them above my head. My neck arches under his lips. "I said I don't mind the hierarchy. Which I don't. But I'm never going to be submissive in bed, Caterina."

He thrusts against me. "Point...taken."

Dom keeps my wrists together as his hand slips beneath the shirt, cupping my breast and rolling my nipple between his fingers. Gray eyes meet mine, heated and possessive as his hand slips down, under the silk of my underwear until he grips my pussy, squeezing lightly. "So fucking wet already."

"Starting without us?" I twist my head to the door as Luc saunters in, his hands in his pockets. He raises an eyebrow as my eyes travel to the others slipping in behind him. "Little crow."

I bite the inside of my cheek to hide my smile.

Domenico shifts until I can't see him, his hands still gripping my wrists. "Spread your legs, Caterina. Show them how wet you are."

Shivering, I do as he says, my thighs spreading wide. Luc strolls to the foot of the bed, his finger reaching out to stroke down the center of my damp underwear. "I see what you mean. Quite the issue."

"No games tonight," I say breathlessly. "I want you. All of you."

All of us together, on our last night here.

Luc slides his hands up my shins, heat traveling in his wake as he meets my gaze. "Shirts on? Or shirts off?"

Biting my lip, I glance around. The lamp beside our bed casts a warm glow over their faces. "Off."

Clothes rustle as they strip, my greedy eyes drinking them in. My eyes flit over the still-red scars marring Luc's stomach, the thin lines on Gio's chest from the beating Matteo gave him.

We could tell our story, beginning to end, through the marks on our bodies.

The bed dips next to me, and I rise up to meet Stefan as his lips caress mine. His fingers grip my chin as he delves into my mouth, tasting and licking until his teeth sink into my lower lip.

Fingers on the buttons of my shirt, undoing them until they push the sides apart, baring my flushed skin.

I gasp into Stefan's mouth as lips press against my underwear, a tongue tracing me through the fabric.

More hands join us. I tear my mouth from Stefan to meet Gio as his hands play with my breasts, tweaking and tugging until my body moves with the demand for more.

Never enough. I will never get enough of these men, never be close enough.

Dom traces his fingers up and down my arm as Stefan leans back first, his dark eyes gleaming. His hand drops from my face to grasp his cock, sliding his hand up and down as he rubs his thumb across the head.

I suck in a breath when he brushes it against my mouth, pushing it in. "Suck, Caterina. Taste what you do to me."

I wrap my lips around his thumb as cool air hits between my legs, Luc dragging my underwear down. My eyes travel down, spot Luc and Dante murmuring as I pull my mouth away. "What are you two planning?"

The smiles they give me curl my toes. Green eyes glitter in the low light as Dante smirks. "You'll find out, *tentazione*."

Dom releases my hands, and I twist to look as he moves opposite Stefan. They both watch me as Gio nudges Dante out of the way. His cock is already in his hands, his eyes on my face as he rubs it up and down my center, gathering the wetness there.

I lift my hips in a silent plea.

Gio slips his hands under my thighs, lifting my hips off the bed as his cock pushes against my entrance. He nods his head. "I'd tell you to watch, but you're going to have your mouth full, Corvo."

I turn as he pushes inside me in one, deep thrust, my mouth opening on a gasp that turns to a muffled moan as Dom pushes his cock inside my mouth.

He taps my cheek. "Suck, baby."

Gio doesn't go slow. He steadily picks up the pace until my body bounces against the bed, held in place by his grip on my thighs. My muffled pants sound around Dom's cock as he pushes it in and out of my mouth, dragging his head across my lips before he grips my hair lightly and pulls me away. "Turn."

Blindly, I turn my head. Another pair of hands slide into my hair as Stefano guides himself to my mouth, sinking into me with a low groan.

My quiet, reserved Asante reaches down to flick at my nipple, twisting and tugging until my eyes are glazed, my mouth and my pussy full as they fuck me. Stefan matches Gio's thrusts, the two of them working me between them.

Stefan reaches down, and my eyes widen as he *pinches my fucking nose closed*. "Swallow me down, Caterina. I want to feel my cock deep in your throat."

He sinks in further as my throat works, taking him as deep as he can get until his pelvis presses against me. Gio's fingers pinch my clit at the same time, Dom's mouth sealing around my nipple as he pins me down.

I *detonate*, my body twisting and clenching and my cry vibrating around Stefano's cock as he comes with a hot rush down the back of my throat. Gio's fingers dig into my hips as he thrusts and holds it, his cock erupting into me until I'm dripping down onto the bed.

Stefan pulls out immediately, his hand cupping my cheek. "You okay?"

Gasping, I blink at him. "No more drinking with Domenico."

He grins at that, and Dom flicks my nipple in recrimination as Gio slowly pulls out. A towel is pressed to me as I sag back into the bed, my body loose and trembling.

"You're not done yet, tentazione."

My eyes fly open. "I'm so done I'm *burnt*."

Their amusement echoes around the bedroom as Luc and Dante lean over me. Dante's lips curl up. "You can lay back. Let us... do the work."

His words draw a frown to my face. "Your back—,"

"Is *fine*." He smirks at me as Luc moves up. "We worked it out."

"What do you mean, you worked it—."

My words cut off as Luc flips me onto my side, sliding in next to me and tugging until I'm laying on top of him, my back to his chest. He presses his lips to my damp neck, his teeth scraping over my skin. "Spread those pretty thighs, little crow."

His knees push up and between my legs, shoving them apart.

"We're going to take this nice and slow." Dante trails his fingers up my leg. "Aren't we, Morelli?"

Luc shifts, and I inhale as the head of his cock pushes into me. "Absolutely."

At this angle, the rungs of his Jacob's Ladder drag against me, making me feel every inch as he slowly sinks inside me. Dante rubs the pad of his thumb over my clit, and my head falls back against Luc's shoulder as he pumps into me slowly.

Dante lifts up my legs, keeping Luc buried inside me as he presses them up to hook over his shoulders. My mouth opens as I watch him notch his cock against Luc's. "Deep breath, *tentazione*."

And he begins to push into my pussy, alongside Luc.

The stretching sensation grows as he pushes deeper, a curse slipping from his mouth. He looks up to meet my eyes, lips parting as he thrusts slightly. "So fucking tight."

"Taking it so well." Luc licks up my neck, his hands moving to my breasts as he squeezes and kneads them. "How does it feel having both of us inside you, little crow?"

My moan ripples through the room. I feel so fucking full, both of them working together to push in and out until my vision blurs, my body tensing against Luc.

"She's getting close." He tugs on my nipples as Dante places his foot on the bed, bending forward as his hand grips my knee.

"I—,"

The clenching in my stomach turns violent, rippling as my entire body begins to tremble, flashes of hot and cold flickering.

"Come for us." Dante scrapes his thumb over my clit before he and Luc pull out and push back in, as deep as they can go. "*Scream* for us, Caterina Corvo."

My cry echoes through the room, the apartment, probably the whole fucking *campus* as I come apart in their arms. Luc shakes against me, his face buried in my hair as he groans my name and jets his releases into me in hot pulses.

Dante drags his cock out, and I watch as streams jet from his cock, coating my clit, my pussy as his eyes travel over my trembling body.

I slump back into Luc, his hand running over my hair as our bodies cling together damply, breathing in sync. Dante sets my legs down and I let them fall, watching through lowered eyes as he stares at my pussy with a satisfied gaze. "Looking a little full of yourself there, V'Arezzo."

He smirks. "And you're looking a little full of me, *tentazione*. So we're both happy."

Yes, I think. I'm ready for a lifetime of this.

A lifetime with them.

Stefan lifts me up, carrying me into the bathroom as I coax him under the spray with me, even though my legs feel like jelly. We finally emerge to a clean bed that I promptly crawl into the middle of.

"We need a rota," I murmur drowsily.

Gio presses himself against my back, his lips on my skin. "We already have one. You think it would be this peaceful if we didn't?"

Oh. Smiling, I bury my cheek into the pillow.

Luc slips in on my other side, a shirt thrown on over his chest as he kisses my forehead. "*Ti amo*, Caterina Corvo."

"*Ti amo*." I breathe the words, drinking in the murmurs that float back to me.

Smiling, I close my eyes.

I have been an heir. A daughter. An enemy. A wife.

I have been many things, but I'm finding that I like this version of myself better.

My name is Caterina Corvo.

Head of the Corvo family.

A little scarred, but stronger for it.

A mama, still learning.

A lover, always.

And *happy*.

STALK ME

Mastery Playlist